THE OUTPOURING
Jesus in the Feasts
of Israel

BY

ELWOOD McQUAID

**THE FRIENDS OF ISRAEL
GOSPEL MINISTRY, INC.**
P. O. Box 908
Bellmawr, NJ 08099

Library of Congress Catalog-in-Publication Data

McQuaid, Elwood.
   The Outpouring.

   1. Bible. N.T. John—Criticism, interpretation, etc.
2. Fasts and feasts—Judaism. 3. Fasts and feasts in
the Bible—Typology. 4. Jesus Christ—Person and of-
fices. I. Title.
BS2615.2.M353 1986 226'.506 85-29866
ISBN 0-8024-6101-8 (pbk.)

4 5 6 7 8 9 10 Printing/VP/Year 94 93 92 91 90

Printed in the United States of America

Contents

Introduction

This book is a departure from the prevailing practice of viewing John's gospel through the sign miracles performed by our Lord. It is not that I question the correctness of reading the apostle's Spirit-given word from such a perspective. I am, however, convinced that there is a dimension in this gospel that has been neglected—one that needs to be emphasized in order for us to properly comprehend the whole of what is being presented in John's treatise.

As one reads the book, he will find that the overwhelming majority of the content is given to Jesus' ministry at the great feasts of Israel. As a matter of fact, of the 879 verses found in John's gospel, more than 660 are directly related to events occurring at these feasts.

The revelation of the God-Man is projected against the typical, ceremonial, and prophetic backdrops hung before us in the Old Testament Scriptures. But that is not all. Jesus Christ came to earth as a Jew—one who lived and ministered in the historical and cultural setting of the Jewish nation. It is through the Messiah's interaction as a Jew that God chose to reveal the rich detail of the fabric into which the divine credentials of the Christ are woven.

Accordingly, we believe, John gives us a three-dimensional look at the Son of God.

1. Christ's inextricable bond with Old Testament types, symbols, and prophetic pronouncements is made manifest through His relation to Israel's feasts. He was at the feasts as the one prefigured in all of the ceremonies.

2. As a result, when one examines carefully the words Christ uttered in relationship to the ceremonies enacted at the feasts, they

take on a new depth of meaning. His words provide the fullest possible drawing aside of the veil to allow a magnificent view of the antitypical ministry of Jesus of Nazareth. While the minds of the people were occupied with the sounds and ceremonies of Israel's great national festivals, Jesus Christ stepped forward to make astonishing statements about Himself, His Father, His relationship to the eternal Word, what they must do about Him, and the consequences of their decision. This intercourse between Messiah, feasts, priests, people, and His followers presents a comprehensive revelation of the implications of the incarnation.

3. The signs (miracles) provide confirmation of His credentials as the one foreshadowed in the symbolism of the feasts. He would not only say He was the "I AM" and one with the Father but would also demonstrate through His miracles that what He said was a fact they must act upon.

This work is not offered as a commentary on the entire gospel but rather as an examination of the implications of the ministry and message of Jesus Christ in concert with Israel's feasts.

In the pages that follow, I have attempted to draw the foregoing considerations together. We will mingle with the people on their journey to Jerusalem to participate in the festive activities. Along the way we will examine their situation culturally, religiously, and emotionally. In so doing we will, it is hoped, come to understand something of what they experienced and how they reacted to this exposure. We shall also take our places beside the disciples to ponder Jesus' words and their responses to His declarations. The maneuvering of the priests, their opposition and final rejection of the Messiah will be seen in the light of what they clearly understood Him to be saying about Himself. Finally, we will stand before the altar to watch and listen as the sacrifices are offered and the ceremonial festivities unfold. Preeminently, however, we will fervently aspire to view Him and the marvelous depth of provision Jehovah has laid before us in Jesus Christ.

In preparation for reading *The Outpouring,* it will be profitable to read John's gospel through at least twice. In the process, mark in your mind those references made to the feasts and the corresponding flow of events.

In order to maintain the flavor of certain narrative passages, I have added some descriptive material not related in the biblical text.

These points will be obvious to the reader. They are not, of course, intended to imply authoritative accuracy.

Great care has been taken to develop these portions in a manner that reflects logical inferences rising from the text and conveys scenes that are culturally and historically correct.

1

Every Man As He Is Able

John 1:1—2:12

Three times a year shall all thy sons
Come to the chosen place;
Worship, tithe and sacrifice
Before Jehovah's face.

The way up to the Temple Mount
One day Messiah trod;
Stood before the gathered throng
That man might see his God.

F ragrant winds of springtime were blowing across the mountains and meadows of Palestine. Their soft persuasiveness had converted the snows of towering Hermon into cascading rivulets that rushed southward toward the Kinneret. There the breezes played over the face of the waters and caused fishing nets to hang in undulating circles before lightly falling to the surface. Along the roads of Israel the gusty freshness ruffled the garments of thousands of pilgrims who were retracing the way to Jerusalem. Fires from the sacrificial altar before which the Passover offerings would soon be sanctified seemed to flash as a beacon to the descendants of Abraham residing in the far reaches of the known world. It was once again time to come for refreshment and renewal within the sacred environs of holy Jerusalem.

From across the river to the east, Jews from Mesopotamia, Elam, Babylonia, Media, Persia, and Parthia journeyed along the great trade route that arced along the Fertile Crescent and then swung south to bring them to their destination. The journey was reminiscent of the one Abraham had taken as he made his way down to the land that the Lord was to show him.

Jewish feet fell upon the ancient road that brought travelers up the dusty way through the barrenness of the Sinai. As they moved out of the shadow of the pyramids, recollections of Jehovah's triumph over a tyrannical pharaoh pressed upon their consciousness.

To the north, frowning legionnaires watched the rush of pilgrims streaming out of the royal city, Rome, to answer the divine summons. Well might Jews who lived under the purple mantle of Tiberius Caesar have entertained cherished thoughts and guarded conversations of the time when the Messiah would reign as true King on the earth. The stream was swollen by Jews from Asia Minor, Africa, and the islands of the sea until the length and breadth of Israel was a variegated tapestry of humanity. Excitement and anticipation gripped the surging multitude. They were in the land of their fathers for a celebration of remembrance and rejoicing.

THREE TIMES IN A YEAR

Motivation for these festive pilgrimages was not simply a sentimental attachment to a place or kinsman. The Chosen People sought the way to the Holy City in response to a higher directive. Their desire was born of a biblical injunction:

> Three times in a year shall all thy males appear before the Lord thy God in the place which he shall choose; in the feast of unleavened bread, and in the feast of weeks, and in the feast of tabernacles: and they shall not appear before the Lord empty: Every man shall give as he is able, according to the blessing of the Lord thy God which he hath given thee. (Deuteronomy 16:16-17)

Jews were specifically enjoined to "appear before the Lord" three times in a year, at the feasts of Passover, Pentecost, and Tabernacles. Bound up in this command were three specific elements:

1. All males were to appear before the Lord.
2. They were not to come empty.

3. Every man was to bring what he was able to give, according to the blessing of God on his life.

Thus the gathering of the people before Jehovah at the great feasts of Israel was multifaceted in purpose. They were to be times of joy and celebration. "And thou shalt rejoice in thy feast, thou, and thy son, and thy daughter, and thy manservant, and thy maidservant, and the Levite, the stranger, and the fatherless, and the widow, that are within thy gates" (Deuteronomy 16:14). The feasts embodied four primary features:

1. *Historical.* Israel was to remember what God had done in the past and to rejoice in His power to deliver.
2. *Agricultural.* The major feasts were touched by some application of the fruits of husbandry and the soil, which kept the realization of the Lord's sustaining benevolence ever before them.
3. *Sacrificial.* Central to all the feasts was the bringing of the sacrifice to lay before the Lord. The priestly, intercessory ministry of the Temple worship drew spiritually hungry Jews to Mount Moriah like a magnet.
4. *Prophetical.* All of the feast days held tokens of future prospects. Israel's sweeping covenantal promises stood in the foreground of the annual assemblages of the Jewish people. At the heart of it all lay the anticipation of messianic fulfillment.

A NATION IN WAITING

As can be readily observed, every provision had been made to meet the ongoing needs of the Jewish people as individuals and a nation in the great feasts of Israel. For the individual, traditional associations, and an awareness of Jehovah's present care, spiritual provision, and future promise all possessed his mind and spirit during the celebrations. Nationally, these were times when a people who were for the most part from other lands returned to fulfill their material obligations to the nation. Their tithes and offerings replenished the Temple treasury and sustained their national way of life.

Therefore, the prominence of the feasts and their importance in the divine scheme of things can hardly be overstated. They were the predominant means through which God chose to receive worship and maintain His nation.

In all, Israel was given seven feasts by biblical decree. Their succession is recorded in the twenty-third chapter of Leviticus.

The first three, Passover (Leviticus 23:5), Unleavened Bread (Leviticus 23:6), and Firstfruits (Leviticus 23:10) all fell within days of one another in the month of Nisan (April). Nisan was the first month of the Jewish religious year. The cycle began with Passover, which was observed on the evening of the fourteenth. Unleavened Bread was celebrated on the fifteenth. Firstfruits were offered on the day after the Sabbath that followed the Passover.

Fifty days were counted from Firstfruits to the Feast of Weeks (Pentecost) (Leviticus 23:16), which fell in the month Sivan (June).

Trumpets (Leviticus 23:24), the Day of Atonement (Leviticus 23:27), and Tabernacles (Leviticus 23:34) closed out the national religious celebrations in Tishri (October). From Rosh Hashanah (Trumpets) to the close of Tabernacles spanned a period of twenty-two days.

Over the years, extrabiblical commemorations also found a place on the Jewish calendar. Hanukkah (Dedication) and Purim are among the most noteworthy celebrated during the period covered by the gospels.

Overriding every other consideration connected with the feasts was that Israel was, in a literal sense, a nation in waiting. Jewish males came before the Lord with their sacrifices and offerings. But the command went beyond this. They were *themselves* to appear before the Lord. That is, each male was to present himself before Jehovah in the appointed place. During the wilderness wanderings and early days in the land it was to be done at the door of the Tabernacle, Israel's Tent of Meeting. Following the establishment of the permanent house of worship, the nation's sons were to present themselves at the Temple in Jerusalem. There the sacrifices about to be offered would be examined with utmost care for any possible imperfection. While worshiper and priest alike were acutely conscious of this procedure, another examination was in progress. At some point in Israel's history, on one of the festive occasions, a singular historical event was to take place. From among the heirs of Abraham, the promised Messiah would step forward and present His credentials before Jehovah, priests, and people.

For centuries, the people came in response to the solemn command. Some bore the evidence of amassed wealth and laid lavish gifts before the ministering priests. Others brought impressive tithes from the produce of their landholdings or contributions from inherited estates. The rich, middle class, and poor came in a procession that seemed to extend into the distant mists of antiquity. The priests watched, the people waited, and Jehovah stood by His promise to send the Redeemer. Then, one day, He came.

Out of the folds of the Galilean hills one joined the jostling throng for the journey to Jerusalem. He came from the inauspicious village of Nazareth—a place that had never produced one noteworthy figure in its history. Tucked away in the heart of the district, Nazareth was not a place frequented by the prominent rabbis of the period. For Judeans, it was scorned as a habitation of the *Am-ha-arets,* country people who, by Judean standards, were considered uneducated. Indeed, when Galileans ventured south, they were often subjected to ridicule because their manner of speaking was interpreted as an evidence of their lack of academic acumen. Nazareth was not only held in low esteem by the brethren to the south, it was also looked upon with disdain by fellow Galileans. Nathanael, who lived in Cana of Galilee, expressed it for Judean and Galilean alike when he responded to word that the Messiah had been discovered. "Can any good thing come out of Nazareth?" (John 1:46). Philip would answer on God's behalf with a single phrase: "Come and see." It was an invitation to discovery—to discover what God had done under their noses in the quiet village set amidst the lush hills and vales just north of the Plain of Esdraelon. He who had stepped from a carpenter's shop would now present Himself in the City of David. There He would place His credentials, which had already been certified in heaven, before the priests and people. The identity of the Messiah was about to be made known.

Jesus of Nazareth came to Jerusalem as a totally unique being. We will recall that Israel's sons were instructed to come to the Temple; they were not to come empty; they were to bring what they were able according to God's blessing. While others brought great substance, He came as one of whom it could accurately be said, "The foxes have holes, and the birds of the air have nests, but the Son of man hath not where to lay his head" (Matthew 8:20). His earthly brethren presented their gifts from the store of material possessions with which God had blessed them. Jesus did not come up to Jerusalem thus prepared. Yet in His person, which He lay before the Lord, He gave what would be blessing and benefit to "all families of the earth."

THE PATTERN OF THINGS TO COME

The unique attributes and essential character of Jesus of Nazareth leap from the introductory paragraphs of the gospel given us through John.

He is called:

The Word (1:1)	The Lamb (1:29)
The Life (1:4)	The Messiah (1:41)
The Light (1:7)	The King (1:49)
The Son (1:18)	The Son of Man (1:51)

This host of appellations opens in the inquiring heart a virtual flood of anticipation. What will the Word say? How will the Life be lived? Upon whom will the Light shine? How will they recognize the Son? What will the Lamb accomplish? Precisely when will the Messiah be fully revealed? Will man receive the King? Will the Son of Man be triumphant? These questions are all answered in magnificent detail in the flow of what is to follow.

John's first words to us are not limited to a series of names of the one for whom the nation had so long stood in waiting. For names, no matter how majestic, are of supreme value only when one comes to understand their role in relationship to objects or persons. To whom was the Messiah to be related and how? In response to this query, the Lord sets seven relationships before us, which should stir us to wonder, appreciation, and the knowledge of our individual potential before Him. Each of these relationships holds out essential preparation for what is to be revealed as Jesus comes to present Himself at the feasts. In actuality, they are God's contextual undergirding of His program for the disclosure of the Messiah.

HIS RELATIONSHIP TO ETERNITY PAST

"In the beginning was the Word, and the Word was with God, and the Word was God" (1:1).

Never has so much been said in so few words. Although John

does not follow the writers of the synoptic gospels (Matthew, Mark, Luke) in presenting the events surrounding the incarnation of Christ, no utterances of Scripture are more vivid, encompassing, or surpassingly beautiful than these. Jesus of Nazareth, who went up to the feast and spoke before the people as no man in all of history had spoken before, was no less than the God who inhabited eternity past. Thus the message and the issue are introduced. Every act, each word, all miraculous activity, and, decisively, man's verdict concerning Him must be weighed in the light of John's transcending declaration.

> The Word was *before creation*—"In the beginning"
> The Word was *beside the Father*—"And the Word was with God"
> The Word *belonged to the Godhead*—"The Word was God"
> The Word *became a man*—"And the Word was made flesh"

John 1:14 sounds the trumpet, calling us to behold God's highest design for His crowning creation, humanity: "And the Word was made flesh, and dwelt among us, (and we beheld his glory, the glory as of the only begotten of the Father,) full of grace and truth." Jehovah's grand design in sending the Word in a veil of flesh is that man might behold the truth of the incarnation; behold the purity of His life; behold His divine glory; behold His glory as the God-Man—that through our beholding Him and, consequently, knowing Him in possessing faith, we might fulfill the purpose for which we were created: to glorify God.

HIS RELATIONSHIP TO THE CREATION

"All things were made by him; and without him was not any thing made that was made" (1:3).

Following the declaration of His deity is an affirmation of His creatorship. "All things were made by him." Jesus' incarnation introduces the sheer wonder that the Creator has taken about Him the garment of a created being and stepped into time as a man—God has invaded humanity. With this revelation before us, a logical succession of consequences comes into play.

As Creator, He holds the right of ownership. Since He is the Creator of all things, it follows that He is rightfully the owner of all He has created. This forever dispels the satanic delusion that lays claim to man's "inherent right" to forge his own destiny. Human- ism, which sees man as the center of everything, is deposed before the realization that we are subjects of the Creator and therefore subservient to Him in all things.

As Creator, He has the right to reign. It is flagrant rebellion for man to declare his independence of God. The Messiah's lordship is not an issue open to debate. It is His absolute right by virtue of His creatorship. Consequently, we are confronted by an unassailable conclusion:

As Creator, He has the right to pronounce judgment on those who refuse His lordship. The reversal of roles that has been so fervently cherished by humanity is incomprehensible—that is, man's placing himself in the position of judgment on God and arbitrarily rejecting accountability to his Maker. Divine creatorship inherently possesses the right of disposition.

In view of these realities and man's consistent lack of responsive- ness to God, a greater wonder is seen.

As Creator, He became a man and provided a solution to the problem of our estrangement from Him. Following the Fall, the Creator had the unchallengeable right to consign rebellious humani- ty to eternal perdition without any attempt to remedy the situation; but He did not. Instead, God, in love, moved toward us through the incarnation.

HIS RELATIONSHIP TO HIS OWN

"He came unto his own, and his own received him not" (1:11).

This is one of the truly imponderable statements in Scripture: He was refused by His own. Gentile empires had already turned away from their Maker to fling themselves into the abyss of paganism. But now the nation chosen to be His witness to a world shrouded in darkness said no to its sovereign. That they did so deliberately, with full access to His credentials as Messiah of Israel, stuns the senses and serves to illustrate the magnitude of mankind's depravity. What follows in the gospel of John not only fully substantiates that Israel's leaders rejected His messiahship, but, in the closing phases of his record, we will also witness the wedding of pagan Rome and priest- ly Israel before the altar at which He was condemned—"despised and rejected of men; a man of sorrows, and acquainted with grief" (Isaiah 53:3).

HIS RELATIONSHIP TO BELIEVERS

"But as many as received him, to them gave he power to become the sons of God, even to them that believe on his name" (1:12).

As certainly as the preceding verse slams the door on the fantasy of man's spiritual integrity, the next throws it open to the resourcefulness of a condescending God. John's exquisite gospel is sent forth that men might lay hold of the tremendous prospects awaiting those who become believers. John expresses this in his summarizing observation: "But these are written, that ye might believe that Jesus is the Christ, the Son of God; and that believing ye might have life through his name" (20:31). Every aspect of the book is bent so that we, having become aware of all sides of the issue, might believe on Him. In John 1:12, God reveals His consuming desire for all men. In it we discover:

Universality— "as many . . ." The remedy is as universal as the disease of sin. Jews and Gentiles find it possible to join hands in a growing body of believers, who, across the centuries, exercise faith in Christ.

Simplicity— "as received him . . ." The consequence of the revelation of the God-Man is the inevitable question: "Will you receive Him?" It is simple, beyond anything human ingenuity could concoct. Yet it is profound, beyond anything man can fully comprehend.

Surety— "gave he power to become . . ." The word *power* carries, in a dynamic sense, the thought of *authority* or *right*. The sovereign Creator has initiated a transference of rights to those who will receive Him. Believers are given the *power, right, authority* to become the children of God. Their assurance is in His ability to secure their sonship—they become children by right of divine commission.

Liberty— "children of God . . ." Believers possess liberty as sons of the King. In the words of another writer of Scripture, Paul, believers experience the "glorious liberty of the children of God" (Romans 8:21). Those who had passed the long night in the bondage of sin and despair, are, through faith, suddenly thrust into the light and liberty that is the permanent possession of the members of His family.

Opportunity— "even to them that believe on his name." John is the gospel of the believer. The riches of Christ's infinite provision are delivered through belief in His name. The opportunity to gather those riches is laid before all men.

HIS RELATIONSHIP TO THE LAW

"For the law was given by Moses, but grace and truth came by Jesus Christ" (1:17).

One of the dominant themes of John's gospel is observed in the above quotation. It will never be fully understood or appreciated until one examines the statement in its historical and cultural context. Jesus' conduct and comments at the feasts dramatically articulate His relationship to the law and the old economy. He is presented as the one who had come to fulfill every requirement it set forth. And whereas His miracles demonstrate His divine power over creation, His fulfilling of the law establishes His divine right to liberate men spiritually and eternally. One should note carefully that John 1:14 emphasizes "grace and truth" as being resident in the "only begotten of the Father." John 1:17 informs us that this "grace and truth" became available to men through Jesus Christ. Availability for man could only be made possible through the work of Christ in meeting fully the demands of the law. The fact is, the law came of age in Jesus Christ. The stern old taskmaster that had laid men low as convicted sinners before a holy God now rose to the noble position of a schoolmaster who unerringly points the way to the Messiah-Savior (Galatians 3:24).

HIS RELATIONSHIP TO JOHN THE BAPTIST

"I am the voice of one crying in the wilderness, Make straight the way of the Lord, as said the prophet Isaiah" (1:23).

John the Baptist was the predicted forerunner of the coming King. His ministry was to be preparatory and introductory. John the Baptist's relationship to the Messiah at once reflects the prophetic aspects of His coming into the world. It is, in one sense, the keynote of John's gospel.

In answer to the priests and Levites, who had been sent by the Pharisees to ascertain who he was, John quoted from an Old Testament passage found in the fortieth chapter of Isaiah's prophecy. The reference was drawn from a portion that stands as a prologue to the closing section of the book. This prologue covers eleven verses, which outline the ministry of the forerunner of the Messiah and then cast a shower of messianic predictions across the sacred page.

> The voice of him that crieth in the wilderness, Prepare ye the way of the Lord, make straight in the desert a highway for our God. Every valley shall be exalted, and every mountain and hill shall be made low; and the crooked shall be made straight, and the rough places plain: and the glory of the Lord shall be revealed, and all flesh shall see it together: for the mouth of the Lord hath spoken it. The voice said, Cry. And he said, What shall I cry? All flesh is grass, and all the goodliness [beauty] thereof is as the flower of the field: The grass withereth, the flower fadeth: because the spirit of the Lord bloweth upon it: surely the people is grass. The grass withereth, the flower fadeth: but the word of our God shall stand for ever.
>
> O Zion, that bringest good tidings, get thee up into the high mountain! O Jerusalem, that bringest good tidings, lift up thy voice with strength; lift it up, be not afraid; say unto the cities of Judah, Behold your God! Behold, the Lord God will come with strong hand, and his arm shall rule for him: behold, his reward is with him, and his work before him. He shall feed his flock like a shepherd: he shall gather the lambs with his arm, and carry them in his bosom, and shall gently lead those that are with young. (Isaiah 40:3-11)

Jehovah's prophetic purpose was to identify the one who would redeem and comfort Israel, and to show how this would come about. The remainder of Isaiah's message is the most compact detailing of the Messiah as Sufferer, Sovereign, and Savior one will find over a comparable span in the Old Testament. In Isaiah's prologue, from which we have quoted, we can observe the fundamental proportions introduced by the prophet. They include:

The revelation of Messiah—"And the glory of the Lord shall be revealed"

The frailty of humanity—"All flesh is grass"

The primacy of the Word—"But the word of the Lord shall stand forever"

Jerusalem, the center of glad tidings—"O Jerusalem that bringeth good tidings"

A cry is to be raised—"Behold your God!"
The Lord God will come—"Behold, the Lord God will come with strong hand"
The Lord will shepherd His people. He will:

"Feed them like a shepherd"
"Gather the lambs with his arm"
"Carry them in his bosom"
"Gently lead those who are with young"

As we observe events in Jesus's life, we will see a thrilling parallel to Isaiah's blueprint for the messianic era. Of course, his prophecies look to the final triumph of the King during the millennial age, but we witness a clear relationship to these predictions in the first-advent ministry of our Lord. These magnificent words provide the biblical foundation upon which the Messiah's offer of Himself as anointed King of Israel would rest. Israel's refusal to receive Him would set in motion the process by which it would be possible to issue the invitation "to as many as receive him." John the Baptist would record it indelibly with his words "Behold the Lamb of God, which taketh away the sin of the world" (John 1:29).

Observant readers will quickly grasp that Isaiah's chronology, like John's, turns almost immediately from the presentation of the reigning King to the servant-sufferer aspects of the Messiah's work. The prophet paints the Messiah as God's "servant" (42:1), who would give His "back to the smiters," His face to "shame and spitting" (50:6), and have "his visage . . . marred more than any man" (52:14). In the fifty-third chapter, Isaiah raises his voice to cry, Behold the Lamb of God, which taketh away the sin of the world.

HIS RELATIONSHIP TO HIS DISCIPLES

"This beginning of miracles did Jesus in Cana, of Galilee, and manifested forth his glory; and his disciples believed on him" (2:11).

Following the miraculous conversion of water to wine at the wedding feast, the record states: "And his disciples believed on him." The point of emphasis drawn from the miracle is placed here and introduces the ministry of Jesus to His followers. It seems we tend to forget that there was always a firm remnant of true believers among the Jewish people. Andrew, Peter, Philip, Nathanael, and their companions were all Jews—Jews who were among a great many who turned to the Messiah of Israel during the days of His earthly witness and work. Although the leaders of the nation rejected Him, the "remnant" spoken of by Paul, another believing Jew, was being called out at this time. As a matter of fact, it was around this Jewish remnant that God began to weave the fabric of His church in which the "middle wall of partition," which had divided Jew and Gentile, was broken down. This fact reemphasizes our need to understand the historical and cultural situations from which His followers came and through which He helped them understand eternal truths about Him. We will be helped in our comprehension of John's gospel if we can identify with these first believers and see events through their eyes.

Observe the pattern of God's working in the lives of Jesus' disciples. His earliest followers had been disciples of John the Baptist. As such, they had accompanied him as he baptized and taught along the Jordan Valley.

> The next day John seeth Jesus coming unto him, and saith, Behold the Lamb of God, which taketh away the sin of the world. This is he of whom I said, After me cometh a man which is preferred before me: for he was before me. (1:29-30)
>
> Again the next day . . . John stood, and two of his disciples; And looking upon Jesus as he walked, he saith, Behold the Lamb of God! (1:35-36)

These statements were made some time after the actual baptism of Jesus by John in the Jordan. Evidence of this is the fact that John speaks of the event in the past tense and also because the forty days of temptation experienced by Jesus were entered upon immediately following His baptism. One can safely conclude that some time had elapsed between the baptism and the disciples' encounter with Christ. What took place during this interval? John himself explains it. "This is he of whom I said . . ." We can be very sure that John, who was specifically sent to prepare the way for the Messiah, was instructing his followers in the identification of the Anointed One. Andrew and his companion seem to have turned to Jesus and followed Him in a natural act of transition resulting from this preparation. How, we may ask, had he gone about preparing them? Obviously through acquainting them with the messianic prophecies of the Old Testament. The mystical air that dominates the thinking of some in regard to Jesus' first contacts with His disciples is not substantiated. These men were prepared to hear Him as a result of the credible testimony of the Word of God. Now the test was whether in word and deed Jesus would meet the biblical standard foretold of the Messiah.

After the Baptist had made his historic announcement of Jesus' being "the Son of God" (1:34), they "heard him [Jesus] speak" (1:37). After pondering His own words, the declaration would be forthcoming, "We have found the Messiah" (1:41).

Thus, two sides of the revelatory triangle were in place: the testimony of the Old Testament and the words of Christ. The triangle was completed at the wedding in Cana of Galilee.

Jesus' first miracle was a confirmation through interaction. "And his disciples believed on him" (2:11). It was not a case of their suddenly awakening to the fact that they were in the company of a man who was capable of performing supernatural acts, but rather that the Messiah's act provided a confirmation of the Old Testament and His own claim of messiahship. Their experience provides the pattern to be followed throughout the gospel of John in the presentation of the God-Man to Israel. The feasts, with their attendant ceremonies and symbols, His words in relationship to them, and the miracles are to be seen sequentially as the Son of God is revealed.

With the preparatory phase of His mission behind Him, Jesus and His disciples turned to face the confrontations awaiting them at Jerusalem.

2
Up to Jerusalem

John 2:13—3:21

Nicodemus heard Him speak
One dark Passover eve.
Shook with deep perplexity
At what one must believe.

Looked he on Messiah's face,
Anointed, Great "I AM!"
Come to suffer, lifted up—
Jesus is the LAMB.

THE FIRST PASSOVER

"**A**nd the Jews' passover was at hand, and Jesus went up to Jerusalem" (John 2:13).

Passover season was a beautiful time of the year in Palestine. Journeying to Jerusalem was particularly pleasant for those who came from the north. For weeks before pilgrims took to the ways, crews had been busy repairing roads and bridges in order to have them ready for the travelers. Sepulchers were carefully whitewashed and stood silent and bright against the dark green fields. This precaution was taken to prevent the possibility of a person's unwittingly coming in contact with a grave and becoming ceremonially defiled, thus becoming disqualified from participation in the feast at Jerusalem. In every village along the way, booths operated under the authority of the high priest were doing a brisk business exchanging the currencies of many lands for the coins used by worshipers to pay the annual Temple-tribute upon their arrival in the City of David. Along the roadways that cut their serpentine courses through the sun-washed hill country, spring flowers danced on the breezes and filled the pilgrims' nostrils with a variety of pleasing aromas.

As the people moved toward their destination, spontaneous bursts of reverent enthusiasm caused the throng to begin singing the Songs of Ascent. These songs, sung to the accompaniment of flutes, were composed from Psalms 120 through 134. Shepherds, who kept lonely vigil over their meandering flocks, heard snatches of the swelling strains that gladdened the heart of every Jew. The words rose as a triumphal song of preparation for entry into the Holy City. "I was glad when they said unto me, Let us go into the house of the Lord. Our feet shall stand within thy gates, O Jerusalem. Jerusalem is builded as a city that is compact together, whither the tribes go up, the tribes of the Lord, unto the testimony of Israel, to give thanks unto the name of the Lord" (Psalm 122:1-5).

Then the valleys reverberated with the majestic chants: "They that trust in the Lord shall be as Mount Zion, which cannot be removed, but abideth for ever. As the mountains are round about Jerusalem, so the Lord is round about his people from henceforth even for ever. . . . The Lord shall bless thee out of Zion, and thou shalt see the good of Jerusalem all the days of thy life. Yea, thou shalt see thy children's children, and peace upon Israel. . . . My soul waiteth for the Lord more than they that watch for the morning: I say, more than they that watch for the morning. Let Israel hope in the Lord: for with the Lord there is mercy, and with him is plenteous redemption. And he shall redeem Israel from all his iniquities," (Psalms 125:1-2; 128:5-6; 130:6-8). And finally, "Behold, bless ye the Lord, all ye servants of the Lord, which by night stand in the house of the Lord. Lift up your hands in the sanctuary, and bless the Lord. The Lord that made heaven and earth bless thee out of Zion" (Psalm 134).

As the echoes of their singing faded into the Judean landscape, all eyes were turned toward the object of their sacred pilgrimage: Jerusalem. It stood above them, brushed by the pink shadows of a retreating sun, with a grandeur no Jew could bring himself to dismiss as commonplace. Some among them had seen Rome, Egypt's Alexandria, Athens, or even far-off Babylon. Each of those cities had its peculiar treasures of which resident sons and daughters could boast as long as men were disposed to listen. But nothing others could talk or sing of compared to what lay before them. This was Jerusalem, and there was no place to equal it on the face of the earth. Jerusalem was the cultural, religious, and emotional center of Jewry; and without question, she held their collective heart fast in her grasp. Quietly, almost as though they were entering a sanctuary, the people quit the roads and moved to residences, hospices, or campsites in or around the city. As they prepared for the night, each joyfully anticipated the experiences the next hours and days would bring.

Jesus' disciples, of course, had been there many times before. Still, as was the case with their kinsmen, they never ceased to wonder at the sights and sounds of the City of David. To be in Jerusalem for Passover was, to say the least, a spectacular adventure. As they pressed through the narrow streets, they must have been all but overwhelmed by the vast numbers of people who were in the city. They found themselves surrounded by a surging sea of humanity. Estimates of the numbers of people attending Passover at this time go as high as 3 million. We are told by reliable sources that more than 200,000 worshipers could be accommodated on the Temple mount at one time. When we realize how many came to Jerusalem for the great national festivals, coupled with the fact that a representation from all segments of dispersed Jewry were in attendance, one can readily understand why Jehovah chose to offer the credentials of the God-Man to the nation at these feasts.

Jesus and His little band moved through the streets to the place of lodging that had been prepared for them. Where they stayed is a matter about which we can only speculate. It has been suggested that on this visit, perhaps He was housed in quarters belonging to the family of John Mark or with Lazarus in Bethany.

A VISIT TO THE TEMPLE

Because of the central relationship of Israel's national house of worship to the events and message of John's gospel, it is important for us to establish a mind's-eye view of the Temple.

If entering Jerusalem brought joy to the hearts of worshipers, the inevitable walk to the Temple mount initiated soul-filling exhilaration. As one entered the city from the southeast on the road from

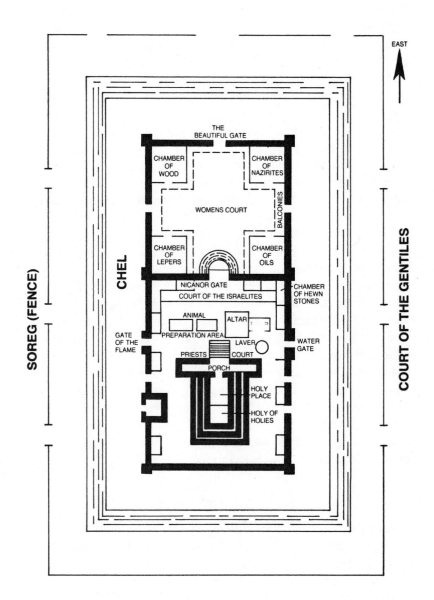

Jericho, past Bethany and along the base of the Mount of Olives, he was afforded a magnificent view of the Temple complex looming high above him. The final ascent was made by way of a road that crossed the Kidron Valley and wound its way up to the Sushan Gate, located on or very near to the now closed Eastern (Golden) Gate. Entering there the visitor found himself standing in a lovely portico, which extended the entire length of the eastern section of the outer wall. This was known as "Solomon's Porch" and was one of four such cloisters encompassing the outer Temple court. Gleaming white stone columns supported the artfully decorated roof above the pilgrim's head. Seats were placed at intervals along this porch. These were used by the rabbis, who taught there. Jesus taught in this area, as did the apostles when believers met in the Temple during the early days of the church. It is conjectured that this may well have been the place where a distraught Mary and Joseph found the boy Jesus questioning the doctors of the law.

The outer walls of the Temple mount enclosed an area Herod had enlarged to approximately three hundred by four hundred yards. The walls were broken by gates providing access from all four sides of the city. Bethesda, a suburb, was situated outside the northern gate. Four entrances came into the court from the west. This allowed people from the Upper City, where Herod's famous palace was located, to enter without undue difficulty. The Tyropoeon Valley, a low depression, which today is filled with debris, ran the length of the western wall and divided the upper and lower sections of the city. At the southwest corner stood a splendid set of steps leading from the flagstone streets up to the south portico. Its remains can be seen today in a stone remnant, "Robinson's Arch," protruding from the wall. Along this western wall was the section now revered as the "Wailing Wall." The Huldah Gates brought worshipers to the Temple from the base of the south wall. These two entrances, one with double and the other having triple openings, were reached from a massive set of steps, which have recently been exposed by archaeologists. From the gates people passed into underground staircases that ascended to openings located roughly in the middle of the southern section of the Court of the Gentiles. It is generally conceded that these gates, coming up from the Lower City (Ophel), were the busiest of all of the approaches to the Temple.

A look to the right from the Eastern Gate revealed a fortress adjacent to the outside of the northwest corner of the wall. It was the Antonia, a Roman garrison that housed troops charged with maintaining order in the city and at the Temple mount. Defense towers stood at each corner of the building. One was considerably higher than the others and served the Romans as an observation post. From it the legionnaires had a commanding view of the entire Temple compound. Two flights of steps descended from the Antonia to the porticos at the northwestern corner of the court providing instant access for the soldiers in the event of a disturbance. It is thought that Roman troops also patrolled the roofs of the porticos during the major feasts. The fortress was more than a garrison for soldiers—it also served as a palace for Roman dignitaries who visited the city. Pilate occupied quarters there when he came to Jerusalem. It was on the lower level of the Antonia that Jesus was condemned by the procurator.

The Court of the Gentiles lay on four sides of the inner Temple enclosure. The court was so named simply because Gentiles were allowed to frequent this area. It was here that the moneychangers and those who sold sacrificial animals located their tables and stalls.

The portico at the south end of the Court of Gentiles is worth our notice. It was a grand exhibition of Herod's genius as a builder. One hundred sixty-two columns, each cut from a single block of stone and standing nearly thirty feet tall, were set four deep along the wall. This "Royal Portico," covered by a roof with an intricately carved cedar interior, rose to a peak 100 feet above the floor of the court. Flavius Josephus, the noted historian of the period, described it as "better than any under the sun." To stand in the Royal Portico and look over into the Kidron Valley hundreds of feet below gave the viewer a spectacular panorama and very often a giddy sensation as well.

Moving across the Gentiles' court toward the inner Temple enclosure brought one to a low stone fence, the Soreg. The partition, about five feet in height, was topped at intervals by notices on stone tablets written in Greek and Latin. They warned Gentiles that they could proceed no farther. To do so was to risk the pain of death.

Beyond the Soreg stood an imposing inner wall. It was, for all practical purposes, a small fortification, protecting the inner courts and buildings of the Temple. The sturdy enclosure had turrets on all corners and at intervals along the walls. Nine gates allowed access to the courts from the north, south, and east. Gates on the north and south had strong doors covered completely with silver and gold plate. The eastern entrance was the "Beautiful Gate," familiar to the readers of the New Testament. Its doors were massive to the extent that it took the combined strength of twenty priests to open and close them. Highly polished Corinthian brass, skillfully worked, plated the gates. The Beautiful Gate was approached by ascending the first of a succession of elevations upon which the Temple and the surrounding courts rested. Fourteen steps led to a Chel, a terrace fifteen feet wide, which went completely around the outside of the inner walls. It was along this terrace that beggars would sit and ask alms. Peter and John had an encounter with a lame beggar who had been placed near this gate. The resulting tumult is recorded in Acts 3-4.

The Court of the Women lay immediately beyond the Beautiful Gate. Women were not the exclusive patrons of this court. As was true in the case of the Gentiles, women were limited in how far they could proceed toward the Temple proper. The women's court was large, with spacious rooms in each of the corners. These enclosures were put to some interesting uses. For example, one was used by Nazirites who had completed their vow of separation. They came here to cut their hair and cook peace offerings. Another chamber was occupied by priests found to be temporarily ceremonially "unclean." They picked insects from the wood to be burned on the altar. Purified lepers had access to one of the rooms. There they prepared themselves for presentation to the priests at the entrance to the Court of the Israelites.

Stairs led up to a balcony that extended along three sides of the women's court. Women would go there to watch proceedings in the other courts. They especially enjoyed their balcony during the Feast of Tabernacles. It was the best vantage point from which to view the priests bringing the golden pitcher of water from the Pool of Siloam for the pouring ceremony at the altar. It was an impressive service, one we will discuss in detail later.

Along the walls beneath the balcony thirteen containers were to be seen. These vessels resembled large trumpets with receptacles attached to their bottoms. Each was labeled and bore a number designating the types of offerings received in the container. The Court of the Women also served as the Temple treasury to which

worshipers came to make their contributions. Vessels marked I and
II were for the half-shekel Temple-tribute and, as one might expect,
were laden with coins at Passover season. Container III will be of
particular interest to us. It was the one in which poor women
deposited money for burnt and sin offerings. The priests would
count the money in the vessel and then offer a corresponding
number of turtledoves of behalf of the women. Our Lord com-
mented on the poor woman casting in her offering as she gave out of
her poverty (Mark 12:41-44; Luke 21:1-4). Jesus' teaching in the
eighth chapter of the gospel of John took place in the treasury (John
8:20).

Fifteen semicircular steps led from the Court of the Women to the
Nicanor Gate. One would almost pause to question which of the two
gates opening to the east was actually the more beautiful. Nicanor
was bronze, lavishly ornamented and set in a superb arch of polished stone. Levites lined these steps during the Feast of Tabernacles to sing the fifteen Psalms of Ascent. Before this gate, also,
cleansed lepers and women coming for purification presented
themselves to the priests. Incidentally, it was also the place where
women suspected by their husbands of unfaithfulness were given the
"waters of bitterness."

The Court of the Israelites was entered through the Nicanor Gate.
Jewish males could come into this area, which occupied a compara-
tively narrow space extending across the width of the compound. A
low stone divider separated the men's court from the Court of the
Priests. On the top of this wall trophies of war taken by the Maccabees were displayed as reminders of the sacrifices and triumphs of
their forefathers. Herod the Great insisted on adding some articles
from his own campaigns. These were reminders that evoked emo-
tions from the Jews of quite another kind than those of the Maccabeans. Jewish men were allowed in the priests' court during the
sacrificial ceremonies. There they laid hands on the heads of their
animals in an act of identification with the sacrifice. The men also
participated in other rituals attendant to the feasts. Within a short
time, one of Jesus' disciples, probably Peter, would enter the Court
of the Israelites holding a lamb in his arms to present on behalf of
our Lord and his fellow disciples.

Commanding the Court of the Priests was the Great Altar. It was
huge—reportedly forty-eight feet square. Priests reached its fifteen

foot height by way of an inclined ramp leading to a platform built around all sides of the altar. Stones used in the construction of the altar were unhewn, that is to say, they were untouched by stonecutters' tools. A funnel, which carried away the blood of the sacrifices, conducted it into a channel that emptied into the Kidron Valley. Two silver receptacles were located at the southwestern corner of the altar for the drink offerings: one received the wine libations; the other the water from the Pool of Siloam offered at Tabernacles. Several stone tables were positioned on the north side of the altar. Near them tethering rings were fastened to the floor. Animals were tied there as they awaited slaughter. The tables were used for preparation of the carcasses.

The Laver stood behind the altar. It, too, was large and held a great volume of water. The Laver rested upon twelve cast brass lions. Twelve priests could be accommodated for their ceremonial washings at one time.

The priests' court, which lay before and around the sanctuary proper, held many rooms for priests' quarters, storage, and the dispositon of functions related to the business of the Temple. However, our purpose does not warrant a detailed examination of the entire area. We will limit ourselves to the mention of one room of importance and another of interest. Adjacent to the Court of the Priests, probably in the southeast corner, was the Chamber of Hewn Stone. The Sanhedrin, which held sway over the religious fortunes of the nation, met here. This would be the room where much of the plotting against Jesus would take place. We shall say more of this later. The area of interest was the chamber that contained the stones placed there from the dismantled altar profaned by the notorious Seleucid, Antiochus Epiphanes, who sacrificed a swine on it when he invaded Jerusalem. These stones could not be discarded, because they were from the great altar. Neither could they be used again, because they had been defiled. So they were stored at the Temple, awaiting the coming of the Messiah, when He would instruct them about how to resolve the problem. The Messiah would soon be on the scene.

The sanctuary proper inspired gasps of awe and admiration. Majestically rising above twelve broad steps of approach, it held total dominance of the mount, Jerusalem, Israel, and the entire world of Jewry. Its monumental square facade had a beauty that almost defied attempts to properly describe it. It would take only a brief glance for any objective observer to declare it to be one of the true wonders of the world. Pure white stones were faced with large, ornamental plates of fine gold. Four giant columns stood like white-clad angelic sentinals across the front of the structure. Each was capped with a richly decorated gold crown that complimented fully the elegance of their surroundings. Even the protective spikes, placed in the cedar roof to keep birds at a respectable distance, were fashioned of gold. Josephus leaves us an eye-witness appraisal of the sight:

> It was covered all over with plates of gold of great weight, and, at the first rising of the sun, reflected back a very fiery splendor, and made those who forced themselves to look upon it to turn their eyes away, just as they would have done at the sun's own rays. But this temple appeared to strangers, when they were at a distance, like a mountain covered with snow; for, as those parts that were not gilt, they were exceeding white. (Flavius Josephus, *Wars of the Jews*)

The Temple facade, which was much larger than the actual dimension of the width of the inner sanctuary, was the work of Herod. He wanted a building worthy in size of the grand style he enjoyed so much. It was, of course, unthinkable to the Jews that any tampering with the size of the Temple itself could be permitted—that was set by biblical decree. Consequently, Herod and the Jewish leaders would strike a compromise with their permitting him to enlarge the facade to a size more to his liking.

Great gold-covered doors guarded the Holy Place. Hanging from the ceiling above them were mammoth clusters of grapes crafted from gold. These hung by golden chains attached to the ceiling. The clusters were constantly enlarged through contributions of people who wished to provide material expressions of their devotion to Jehovah. Inside the Holy Place stood the Table of Showbread, the seven-branched Candelabrum, and the Altar of Incense. Here the priests ministered daily, carrying out the sacred functions of Jewish worship.

Once each year, on the Day of Atonement, Israel's high priest went behind the Veil into the Holy of Holies to sprinkle sacrificial blood on behalf of the nation. The lamb died that the representative of the people might secure atonement for their souls. This, we know, was repeated faithfully each year, as the people awaited the day when "a more excellent sacrifice" would be offered. For not through "the blood of goats and calves, but by his own blood he entered in once into the holy place, having obtained eternal redemption for us" (Hebrews 9:12). The Lamb of God would soon walk through the courts of Israel's holy house.

MY FATHER'S HOUSE

"And [he] found in the temple those that sold oxen and sheep and doves, and the changers of money" (John 2:14).

When Jesus and His disciples entered the Court of the Gentiles, they came upon a scene totally incongruous with the spiritual solemnities worthy of the house of God. Having stayed in the city the previous night, it is likely that they entered by a staircase from one of the Huldah Gates or through one of the entrances on the western side of the mount. In either case, they passed abruptly from the flagstone streets of Jerusalem into a court scene more reminiscent of a metropolitan shambles than a place of worship. As a matter of fact, the Court of the Gentiles had been turned into "the Bazaars of the sons of Annas"—a Temple market. Moneychangers' tables lined the porticos, and strident voices rang through the court as people haggled over rates of exchange for foreign currencies. There was a rather curious practice in vogue at the time by which the moneychanger's rate of profit increased in direct proportion to the amount of change he was obliged to return to the worshiper. At times, when these exchanges became overheated, Temple guards, Levites appointed to keep order, would rush in with sticks and give some miscreant son of Jacob a quick lesson in how to enjoy the privilege of lining priestly pockets. Sacrificial animals—sheep, doves, and oxen—were available at a price. These animals, which were also sold at stalls located on the Mount of Olives, had been duly inspected and pronounced acceptable for ceremonial purposes. Those who brought their own animals for sacrifice were required to employ the services of a Mumcheh ("approved one") to inspect and declare them Levitically clean. There was, of course, a fee for this service.

The galling thing about the prevailing situation was not isolated in the fact that they had turned the Court of the Gentiles into a marketplace. As if this were not enough, the priests became wantonly guilty of transgressions that could not escape the rebuke of God. These offenses were compounded by blatant abuses that were, in the final analysis, little better than thievery. It was the resident priesthood who garnered immense profits from the sales and services at the Temple. Reaping the greatest benefits were the relatives of the high priest, at this time the sons of Annas. One of these sons was described by Josephus as being "a great hoarder up of money." The Jewish Talmud makes a figurative lament about them as it has the Temple crying out against them: "Go hence, ye sons of Eli, ye defile the Temple of Jehovah!"

Their avaricious conduct was glaringly evidenced in their treatment of the poor. Many of these people were less self-asserting than some of their brethren and were, as a consequence, abused the more. Prices of doves, most frequently offered by the very poor, were raised exorbitantly. Other charges regularly levied on the poor amounted to a variety of forms of extortion. But the poor were not the only targets for their greed. Even the nonresident priests who came at appointed times from their villages to serve at the Temple were exploited by this element. As a result, a deep cloud of resentment and hostility darkened the minds of the people against these unholy custodians of divine things.

"And when he had made a scourge of small cords, he drove them all out of the temple, and the sheep, and the oxen; and poured out the changers' money, and overthrew the tables; and said unto them that sold doves, Take these things hence; make not my Father's house an house of merchandise" (John 2:15-16).

Jesus stood in silence for a time, surveying the activities going on about Him. The disciples must have grown apprehensive as they watched their Master's face. Something was rising there they had never witnessed before, and they were at a loss to know quite what to expect next. He left them and walked to one of the stalls where He obtained some small cords used to tether the animals. As His followers watched, He deliberately fashioned a scourge from the cords. The noises of the court—arguing, abusing, haggling—seemed to become much louder as they glanced about and waited. They stood silent among the pillars as He strode toward the area where the animals were kept. All eyes where suddenly riveted on Him as the uproar caused by scrambling animals and fleeing keepers clattered through the court. Moneychangers backed away from their tables with contorted expressions of dismay as Jesus moved along the portico upending their tables and sending containers of coins ringing across the pavement.

The tumult brought Temple guards rushing across the court, while the Roman legionnaires on watch at the Antonia looked down on the proceedings. Guards quickly summoned their superior, the Captain of the Temple, who in turn called for the Sadducean authorities. They reached the scene as Jesus admonished the dove sellers: "Take these things from here; make not my Father's house an house of merchandise."

People emerging from the Huldah passages found themselves standing in the midst of a tension-charged situation. Here and there, lambs bleated softly as they wandered unattended among the upturned tables and debris created by Jesus' action. All of this was forgotten for the moment, however, because the focus of attention was fixed on the Galilean who was now surrounded by a large crowd gathered at one end of the court.

An assortment of Pharisees, priests, Sadducees, scribes, and Temple guards formed a semicircle around Jesus. Chins quivered in anger as they shook fingers of outrage and flung accusations in His direction. Behind them, disheveled moneychangers, who had been forced to scramble among the people in an attempt to retrieve some of their coins, shouted for redress. Likewise, the men who sold animals, those who were not pursuing them over the Temple mount, were voicing their complaints. Jesus' disciples were standing somewhat apart, waiting to see what would happen. Incredibly, it seemed to them, no move was made to apprehend their Master. It was not that the authorities did not wish to do so. Indeed, one of the prime sources of their rage was found in the fact that they were for the moment helpless. The reason rested in the scores of faces turned toward the rabbi from Galilee. Jesus' act had been immensely satisfying to the people who had been callously misused by the men who now accused Him. In their minds the event had been long overdue, and their hearts pumped with a potentially volatile determination to see this trafficking brought to a halt. To move against Him then would have been a grave tactical error, and no one was more aware of that than the leaders.

It is interesting that their response to His action made no reference to what He had done. Their silence reflects the fact that any forceful reaction on their part might precipitate a popular uprising by the people. Their remonstrance was framed in a question: "What sign showest thou unto us, seeing that thou doest these things" (2:18*b*). In other words, they requested a demonstration that would satisfy them as to the source of His authority. Did He do this by God-vested empowerment? The people pressed forward and listened intently, awaiting His reply.

"Destroy this temple, and in three days I will raise it up" (John 2:19*b*).

A murmur ran through the crowd as the religious leaders conferred in guarded tones. What could He possibly have meant? His reply to the question was, to their minds, patently ludicrous. "Forty and six years was this temple in building, and wilt thou rear it up in three days?" (John 1:20). To this Jesus made no reply. The men turned to one another and then toward the people. But finding no encouragement for their intentions in the faces around them, they walked away, gesturing and shaking their heads.

Israel's Messiah had in fact answered their question. He had identified the one sign before which all other signs to be performed would bow in subservience. It was to be the singular event upon which their ultimate personal decisions must turn—He had emphatically affirmed His coming resurrection. This is not speculation. John pointedly informs us: "But he spake of the temple of his body" (John 2:21). The next verse emphasizes the disciples' future awareness of history's central fact. "When therefore he was risen from the dead, his disciples remembered that he said this unto them" (John 2:22). This sign would surpass all others offered to the leadership of the nation. It would be the sign confirming all He was about to lay before them. Sadly, for many of them, it was a sign that would finally expose the calamitous depths of their resolute unbelief.

One might ask why Jesus did not make this clear to His accusers. First, and most obviously, they did not ask for an explanation. They had what they wanted. Jesus, in their view, had placed Himself in a position that was certain to discredit Him. He was, they thought, caught on the horns of an absurdity—one they felt they could, and later did, use against Him (Matthew 26:61). Failure by Israel's spiritual leaders to pursue the question leads to a telling conclusion: their hearts and minds were not open to an unbiased consideration of

His messianic credentials. We must note this carefully.

At no time during the course of His ministry did they objectively examine His claims. An adversary situation prevailed from the outset—they would never yield. Even in the face of reasoned appeals for moderation set forth by earnest men like Nicodemus (John 7:50-52) they remained adamant. Another conclusion is equally obvious. Knowing their motives as He did, Jesus did not press His claims upon them. He declared His authority in a single statement that was as dark to their minds as the intents of their hearts were toward Him. To the majority of these men, this sign and all of the others stand against them as emblems of their condemnation. Their going away at the dawning of the public exhibition of His messiahship was an act symbolic of the forfeiture of their responsibility to God, truth, and a heart-hungry nation.

As the people slowly drifted from the court and sullen moneychangers rearranged their tables, words that would later come to the minds of the disciples seemed to linger above the scene. It was a phrase from the Psalms: "The zeal of thine house hath eaten me up." The words were reminiscent of something a twelve-year-old boy had said to His worried parents on another Passover in this same place years before. "[Knew] ye not that I must be about my Father's business?" (Luke 2:49). The God-Man was indeed about His Father's business.

John's quotation was the first half of Psalm 69:9. In the context of the confrontation in the Court of the Gentiles, the remainder of the prophecy cast a somber shadow, which lengthened until it fell across a skull-shaped promontory outside the walls of Jerusalem—"and the reproaches of them that reproached thee are fallen upon me" (Psalm 69:9b). Those who had refused to obey the Father's word had turned their ridicule and scorn toward the Father's Son (the Word in flesh). If the disciples were impressed by His zeal for the Father's house, one wonders if other words from the same psalm were passing through the Savior's thoughts: "I am become a stranger unto my brethren, and an alien unto my mother's children" (Psalm 69:8).

"Now when he was in Jerusalem at the passover, in the feast day, many believed in his name, when they saw the miracles which he did. But Jesus did not commit himself unto them, because he knew all men, and needed not that any should testify of man; for he knew what was in man" (John 2:23-25).

During the feast days Jesus performed signs calculated to display His divine ability before them. We are not told the nature of these miracles, simply that many of the people believed when they witnessed these works. It is noteworthy that the Jewish religious leaders did not respond affirmatively to these signs, which they themselves had requested. Further, one is confronted by the seemingly odd note informing us that "Jesus did not commit himself" to the would-be believers. This was, in the words of Scripture, "because he knew what was in man." The credulous multitude related to a man who performed incredible acts, without laying hold on the true substance of either the man or His mission. Theirs was not a response born out of a desire by deeply convicted sinners to be reconciled to God. Their professed enlistment as followers was, on the contrary, an expression of their viewing Him as an instrument available to satisfy their temporal wants and one who might be used to achieve their own ends.

Futhermore, the observant mind will see in Christ's reaction something that will at once mark the quality and purpose of His ministry. Although at this first public Passover feast He was deliberately laying the foundation for all that was to follow, He resolutely resisted the obvious opportunity to exploit their uncomprehending belief in order to promote His divine cause. Note it well, for we need desperately to see and emulate it today—Jesus Christ never manipulated people to achieve His ends, even when they clamored for Him to do so. His signs were a verification of His identity but only guideposts to His truth. The truth in Christ was what He was *declaring*. A fixation with the signs would never do.

PASSOVER

Passover held the distinction of being the first national religious feast of the Jewish people. Not only did it occupy the first place on the religious calendar, but it predated in its establishment all of the other feasts as well. It also marked a singular milestone in the nation's history—Israel's deliverance from Egypt. The initial significance of Passover related to three primary factors, which would shade and shape the national destiny of Israel thereafter.

1. *Deliverance from judgment through the lamb.* This accomplished their *salvation*. The blood of the slain lamb prevailed for the firstborn through God-instituted substitution.

2. *Deliverance from the enemy.* This accomplished *sanctification,* an operation by which Jehovah delivered them from the grasp of Pharaoh and brought them into a relationship requiring complete dependence on Him. They were a nation set apart to the purposes of God.

3. *Deliverance to enter the land.* This forecast their *destination.* The divine design for His chosen people would culminate in their occupation of the Promised Land—"And it shall come to pass, when ye be come to the land which the Lord shall give you, according as he hath promised" (Exodus 12:25). Inherent in this declaration was their final possession of all of the promises to be delivered through Israel's reigning Messiah.

The history of Israel's first Passover set the pattern for its perpetual observance. The record of the event is found in Exodus 12.

A new beginning—"This month shall be unto you the beginning of months: it shall be the first month of the year unto you" (Exodus 12:2). Passover brought a national new birth to Israel. They were entering into a totally new era.

A lamb selected—"Speak ye unto all the congregation of Israel, saying, In the tenth day of this month they shall take to them every man a lamb, according to the house of their fathers, a lamb for an house" (Exodus 12:3). In the face of imminent judgment, God commanded the people to select "a lamb for an house." It was required by Jehovah.

A lamb scrutinized—"Your lamb shall be without blemish, a male of the first year: ye shall take it out from the sheep, or from the goats: And ye shall keep it up until the fourteenth day of the same month" (Exodus 12:5-6). The lamb was to be obediently selected and properly inspected. Every precaution was to be taken. It had to be the right lamb, and the lamb had to be perfect.

A lamb slain—"And the whole assembly of the congregation of Israel shall kill it in the evening. And they shall take of the blood, and strike it on the two side posts and on the upper door post of the houses, wherein they shall eat it" (Exodus 12:6-7). No other means was acceptable. The blood shed and properly applied would alone avail.

A lamb sufficient—"And if the household be too little for the lamb, let him and his neighbor next unto his house take it according to the number of the souls; every man according to his eating shall make your count for the lamb. And they shall eat the flesh in that night, roast with fire, and unleavened bread; and with bitter herbs they shall eat it" (Exodus 12:4, 8). There was to be enough for all, and all were to partake. Theirs was to be a glorious fellowship as they rested in the assurance of the lamb and feasted together on the lamb. Unleavened bread was there to remind them of their haste in leaving the place of bondage and servitude. Bitter herbs were a sufficient remembrance of their suffering.

A lamb saving—"And the blood shall be to you for a token upon the houses where ye are; and when I see the blood, I will pass over you, and the plague shall not be upon you to destroy you, when I smite the land of Egypt" (Exodus 12:13). God's word was their comfort; God's lamb was their deliverance.

A lamb sustaining—"And this day shall be unto you for a memorial; and ye shall keep it a feast to the Lord throughout your generations" (Exodus 12:14a). Israel's spiritual sustenance was in the perpetuating of the ordinance.

A lamb suggesting—"Ye shall keep it a feast by an ordinance for ever" (Exodus 12:14b). Prophetic overtones flow from the command to keep it forever. It is clearly suggestive of the fact that there was to be an antitype in Israel's future. One day, the Lamb would replace the lambs.

When one approaches the subject of Passover as it was celebrated at the time of Christ he should be cognizant of some important considerations. Passover was not an isolated occurrence but rather a ceremony that held a central position in a season of celebration incorporating several important observances. As a matter of fact, Passover was often referred to as a feast of eight days. Of the activities participated in by celebrants, five predominate.

THE PASCHAL LAMB AND THE SEDER

The Passover lamb stood apart in Israel's sacrificial economy. It was like, yet unlike, the other sacrifices. Alfred Edersheim notes: "It was neither exactly a sin offering nor a peace offering, but a combination of them both." Israel's paschal lamb was a kind of summary expression of all that the sacrificial system projected prophetically. Although every sacrifice and ceremony set forth a particular aspect of the Messiah's person and ministry, it is Passover that is singled out as the unifying typical illustration: "For Christ, our Passover, is sacrificed for us." There is a sense in which all other sacrifices were taken as grafts from Passover and rooted into the trunk of Levitical typology. There can be no serious question as to the dominance of the lamb at the sacred seder celebration. All Israelites were to be represented in the sacrifice and covered by its atoning properties. All were likewise to join around the table to memorialize the historical aspects of the feast and partake of the lamb slain as their substitute.

UNLEAVENED BREAD

For seven days, beginning on the night of Passover, Jews ate unleavened bread. The emphasis of the practice was not to be seen in their remembering Israel's affliction by the Egyptians but in her deliverance from the bondage suffered in that country (Exodus 12:17). They feasted on the bread of God's deliverance from *suffering, servitude,* and *death*—it was the bread of a new life. Egypt's leaven had been searched out and destroyed (Exodus 11:15). An interesting question has been raised as to whether Christ's cleansing of the Temple took place on the eve of Passover, when every household in Israel was being purged of the substance that in the Bible is typical of sin.

Israel was at one and the same time "brought forth" by Jehovah and "thrust out" by her enemies (Exodus 12:39). And so this setting apart had made Israel a "new lump," which was separated unto God. The feast, therefore, became a celebration of *life, liberty,* and the *pursuit of their divine destiny.*

Another factor was present in Israel's commemoration of Unleavened Bread. For while there was rejoicing over their being "brought out," there was also the consideration of the supreme objective purposed in their deliverance. Israel was "brought out" to be "brought in." Deuteronomy 6:23 explains: "And he brought us out from thence, that he might bring us in, to give us the land which he sware unto our fathers." Consequently, the feast hailed God's deliverance to *devotion, dedication,* and *preparation* for the task before them in entering the land to possess their possessions and make ready for the coming of the Messiah and the establishment of His theocratic kingdom.

FIRSTFRUITS

Offering firstfruits involved national and individual participation. The national observance was held at the Passover season. Priests from the Temple were sent into a designated field across the Kidron Valley with instructions to reap the first sheaf of the new barley harvest, which had been carefully chosen and tied in preparation for the ceremony. Following a prescribed ritual, the priest thrust in the sickle and gathered the symbolic sheaf. The ripened grain was taken to the Temple where, on the following day, it was waved before the Lord in a service of dedication and thanksgiving for the representative sheaf that assured a harvest would follow. Until this ceremony was consummated, no new barley could be sold in the land.

Individual firstfruit offerings were brought later, during a period that began at Pentecost and formally closed with the celebration of the Feast of Tabernacles. These offerings were presented with a confession described in Deuteronomy 26:1-11. There is to be found in firstfruits an almost irresistible digression, one which, unfortunately, we must pass with only a comment. Scripture tells us that the national observance typifies Christ as the firstfruit guarantee of resurrection life to the millions of believers who came after Him. "But now is Christ risen from the dead and become the firstfruits of them that slept" (1 Corinthians 15:20). Individual firstfruits began to be presented at Pentecost, the very day the Holy Spirit empowered the church to deliver the message of resurrection life to men the world over. They continued to be offered until Tabernacles, which corresponds to the regathering of Israel—following the resurrection of the saints—and the establishment of the kingdom of Jesus Christ.

BURNT OFFERINGS

Rabbinical instruction for the period in which Jesus went up to Jerusalem directed that a burnt offering be sacrificed on one of the feast days during the Passover season (see Leviticus 1:1-17). As was ever the case, the burnt offering was emblematic of substitution. The particular emphasis of the rite, however, rested on the voluntary aspect of the offering. It stood symbolically for a willing total surrender to God. Isaac provided a sublime type of the concept when he was taken to Moriah as "a burnt offering" (Genesis 22:2) and willingly subjected himself to Jehovah (Genesis 22:7-8).

PEACE OFFERINGS

The peace offerings laid before the Lord at Passover were expressions of joy and fellowship with God. The offering itself is described in Leviticus 3:1-11 and 7:11-21. It was always to be the final offering brought by worshipers during the festive season and reflected the praise-filled spirit of one who was both *justified* and *accepted* by Jehovah. Thus the penitent sinner was at peace with God. Peace offerings consisted of the sacrificial animal accompanied by appropriate meal and drink oblations. Meal offerings were brought in the form of baked loaves, which were represented on behalf of the worshiper by the priests. The offerings of wine were poured out at the base of the great altar.

In view of the multiple activities of the Passover season, one can better appreciate how the Temple must have been constantly crowded with people who were fulfilling their obligations to God, and, more significant, grasp the rich symbolism from which the Messiah molded His declarations of the fulfilling antitypical aspects of His divine person and work.

"BIND THE SACRIFICE"

The first Passover recorded in John's gospel can be reconstructed. On the night of the thirteenth of Nisan those who were responsible for preparing the room where the Lord and His disciples would share the seder joined other Jewish householders in the annual search for leaven. Men with small candles in hand went through the houses looking for anything that held the defiling substance. All leaven found by the searchers was laid aside awaiting the signal to burn it. The exact time this was done was determined through the disposition of two leavened loaves placed by the priests on a bench in one of the porches at the Temple. When the first one was removed, the people were to abstain from eating leaven. With the disappearance of the second, burning of the leaven was to begin.

In the late afternoon of the fourteenth of Nisan, following the slaying of the evening sacrifice, about 2:30 P.M., men bearing their lambs gathered at the Temple. Jesus' disciple, or quite possibly two of them, joined the dense crowds moving toward the Court of the Priests in anticipation of the service. Inside, white-robed priests and Levites made ready to receive the worshipers. Pilgrims were divided into three sections and ushered into the court according to these divisions. Upon entering, the massive Nicanor Gates were closed behind them, and a three-fold blast from the priests' trumpets signaled the commencement of the ceremony. The lambs were slain by the worshipers, who were arranged in two rows across the court, and the blood caught in golden bowls held by priests standing before them. It was passed up to the altar for application and pouring.

While the sacrifices were being made, Levites lifted their voices in the singing of the Hallel. The Hallel is composed of Psalms 113 through 118. Space prohibits an examination of the full text of these psalms, but the reader should become familiar with them—they are of major significance. Psalm 113 is a song of praise to Jehovah. The next celebrates Israel's deliverance from idols. Psalm 116 gives praise for deliverance from death, and the closing portion, 117 and 118, raises thanksgiving for the Lord's saving goodness. The immense prophetic implications resident in the Hallel, which was also sung in all Jewish homes at the close of the seder, will be considered when we observe how Jesus employed them. Just now, however, it is important to note what the Talmud, through its Jewish writers, says regarding the message of these psalms. It proposes that the Hallel sets forth five things: "The coming out of Egypt, the dividing of the sea, the giving of the law, *the resurrection of the dead, and the lot of the Messiah.*" According to this view, Psalm 116 is related to resurrection, and Psalm 118 is seen in a messianic context. This observation tallies precisely with the Messiah's sacrifice, resurrection, and power to deliver, which, as we have seen, is so much a part of the ceremonialism of Passover, Unleavened Bread, and Firstfruits.

Worshipers joined in the singing by repeating the first line of each psalm and then interjecting praise responses at designated places in the passages. As the singing reached the climactic words of 118, the disciples, priests, and people intoned in unison three lines of the closing section:

> Save now, I beseech thee, O Lord!
> O Lord, I beseech thee, send now prosperity!
> Blessed is he that cometh in the name of the Lord!

When the singing died away, the lambs were washed and the portions to be offered on the altar separated and prepared for burning.

The representatives of Jesus and their fellows then departed the Temple carrying the lamb on a stave between them toward the place where it would be roasted and brought to the Passover table.

All was in readiness when Jesus and His followers climbed the steps to the room in which they would gather around the lamb and partake of the initial Paschal Feast of His public ministry. We will forgo discussing the meal itself until the final Passover. Let it suffice, at this point, to leave the scene contemplating how fully our beloved Savior became the Passover Lamb.

THE NIGHT VISITOR

A blustery wind played along the darkened street as a man, obviously in a hurry, made his way toward the upper room where Jesus was lodging. In his mind he was carefully framing an introductory statement. It must, he thought, immediately communicate his sincere desire to know exactly who the Galilean was and the essential nature of His mission. Nicodemus knew that his being a member of the Sanhedrin might cause Jesus to be on His guard. Because of this possibility, he believed it best to establish that he was not cut from the same cloth as his vociferous contemporaries, who were opposing the work of the rabbi from the north. To be sure, it was risky business for the questioning Pharisee to be making this night visit. But he was compelled by an irrepressible inner urging to have an answer to the questions that had dominated his thinking since he had listened to Jesus teach and observed what He was doing.

Many commentators and preachers owe Nicodemus an apology for the way he has been defamed as one exhibiting skittish tendencies by coming to the Messiah after darkness had fallen. Timidity may well have been a part of the man's nature, but calling him a coward is not a fair appraisal of his character. For when one begins to comprehend the tremendous prejudices Nicodemus suppressed in coming to Jesus at all, he will see him as a man who possessed a rather remarkable degree of courage. Not only so, but his act should put to rest our disposition to write off all Pharisees as unprincipled hypocrites and scoundrels. Although there were without question those who richly deserved the scathing denunciations heaped upon them by our Lord, there were also men among them who had a hunger for God and were responsive to the truth that was placed before them in Jesus Christ.

Although the party was relatively small—estimates tell us that there were probably no more than six thousand Pharisees in Jesus' day—their power and prestige among the people was obvious. The central tenets of Pharisaism were exhibited in their preoccupation with piety and learning. Strict obedience to the observances and ordinances insuring Levitical purity and the paying of tithes and dues were among the pillars of pharisaic discipline. They were separatists in the extreme; therefore they took great pains not to defile themselves through contact with Gentiles, the Levitically unclean, or the unlearned common people. The party played an important role in national life through two institutions, the Temple and the synagogue. Members served in the Temple priesthood and sat on the supreme ruling Jewish body in Israel, the Sanhedrin. Their primary strength, however, was not exercised through the agency of the Temple, which was, for the most part, under the control of the Sadducees. As a matter of interest we should note that the Sadducees' power base was so bound to their association with the Temple that the party ceased to exist after the destruction of the Temple in A.D. 70.

Controversy between the two parties was constant. Whereas Pharisees claimed to derive their authority from holiness and study, Sadducees held that superiority came through genealogy and position. Consequently, the Sadducees were aristocratic hellenists who tended to stand aloof from the people and stay in rather close proximity to the Temple and Jerusalem. Pharisees, on the other hand, chose to concentrate their efforts in the synagogue. There they placed great emphasis on worship, study, and prayer. Their proximity to the people in the towns kept them in the public eye and served to enhance their influence. In the course of time the Pharisees raised the synagogue to a position of supreme importance among the Jewish people.

Pharisees believed in both the written and oral law. This meant that although they professed implicit belief in the writings of Moses (the Torah), they also held that the law was supplemented and explained by both the writing prophets and unwritten tradition. The law was to be understood in the light of interpretation by the rabbis who, they believed, were endowed by God with the ability to communicate divine truth. This conviction resulted in the development of a great body of tradition, which eventually obscured the Word of God and was, consequently, condemned by our Lord. Additionally, they believed in the resurrection of the dead; a coming day of judgment, reward, and retribution in the life after death; and the appearance of the Messiah. Pharisees leaned in the direction of predestination and saw it touching all areas of life. This was held by many of them to the point of fatalism.

Pharisaism was known for its degrees and extremes. On the one hand there were those who, because of their punctilious observance of the traditional rituals, bordered on becoming public nuisances. This type of Pharisee was at once recognized by his dress and manner. He would wear wide blue borders and elaborate fringes on the lower part of his white outer garment. At the appointed time for prayer he would stop wherever he happened to find himself—frequently in the most inappropriate places—even, it was said, "if a serpent were winding around one's heel." The Pharisee would pull his feet together and bend forward until his body assumed a contorted position. A pained expression marked his facial features as he began to recite his prayers. Long prayers were thought to possess special virtue. "Much prayer," they believed, "was sure to be heard." The consequences of their street-corner ostentation was the ridicule that came from many of their fellow citizens.

At the other end of the spectrum stood men like Nicodemus—men of piety with reason, men who were sensitive to the need for divine light that would satisfy what barren ritualism could not.

"Rabbi, we know that thou art a teacher come from God; for no man can do these miracles that thou doest, except God be with him" (John 3:2).

In a quiet guestchamber in Jerusalem, responding to the initial words of the inquiring Pharisee, the God-Man was to enlarge on Philip's eloquent invitation to the reluctant Nathanael, "Come and see." Nicodemus had come and would hear that evening the sublimest words yet to fall on the ear of man. He did not "see" immediately but had laid before him a revelation of the Father's provision in fulfillment of the messianic promises in the Old Covenant. Jesus' conversation with Nicodemus gives us an equally brilliant exhibition of His identification of the final Lamb, who personified all that was prefigured in the typological sketches drawn in the ceremonialism of the Passover.

"Except a man be born again, he cannot see the kingdom of God" (John 3:3).

Jesus' reply to the Pharisee's query was startlingly direct and designed to thrust into the mind of Nicodemus the immense proportions of the proposition being opened to him. The analogy is unmistakable. Israel's first ancient Passover brought a "beginning of months" to the people who were at the time experiencing a national birth. The sound of the taskmaster's lash was being drowned out by Israel's song of deliverance. The Passover Lamb, the sheltering blood, escape from judgment, the fiery pillar, and the triumphal procession through the sentinal waters of the Red Sea combined to herald a new era—a new birth.

Now Jesus turned the focus down from the national reality, with which His guest was well acquainted, to an individual necessity: "Ye must be born again." And suddenly the ultimate divine purpose, which had for so long been shaded by a national and historical veil, burst before him in the light of Jesus' clarifying word. The birth of the nation was but a symbol for God's higher design in providing for the birth of a soul.

The light was too bright for the wondering Pharisee. He must have furrowed his brow, stroked his beard, and turned these words over for a considerable period of time before he looked up in resignation. "How can a man be born when he is old? Can he enter the second time into his mother's womb, and be born?" (John 3:4). His reply mirrored the abject spiritual density that had immersed Pharisaism in external, superficial nit-picking and blinded them to the spiritual richness of the symbolism and messianic predictions of the Old Testament. His answer sprang from the popular frame of reference: the physical and time-shackled.

The birth from above introduced by Jesus Christ surpassed by eternal light-years his dwarfed spiritual comprehension. Jesus patiently explained the fact that as there was a physical birth, so must there be a spiritual birth: "That which is born of the flesh is flesh; and that which is born of the Spirit is spirit. Marvel not that I said unto thee, Ye must be born again" (John 3:6-7). At this, Nicodemus's mind was surging with a question he would articulate momentarily. Before he could speak, Jesus was speaking again. "The wind bloweth where it listeth, and thou hearest the sound thereof, but canst not tell whence it cometh, and where it goeth: so is every one that is born of the spirit" (John 3:8). When Jesus finished, Nicodemus blurted out his bewilderment: "How can these things be?" (John 3:9). The Messiah gently rebuked His learned visitor and began to speak words that must have seemed to Nicodemus too wonderful for human ears to hear. They were words that would possess his mind and spirit in the days to come and eventually lead him to the light.

As the rabbi-turned-student pondered his teacher's rebuke, Jesus lay before him a preamble to His central declaration (John 3:11-13). He began by saying, "We speak that [which] we do know, and testify that we have seen." Here Jesus emphatically identified Himself with Moses and the prophets as the transmitter of eternal truth, thus the union of His word with the words of the prophets. But His statement must also pass beyond the human communicators to the source of truth Himself, Jehovah. For He set forth the certainty—"know" and "have seen"—of an eye-witness.

Then He continued by dispelling the rabbinical notion that Moses had ascended into heaven to receive the law. "No man hath ascended up to heaven." On the heels of this eye-opening word, Jesus declared this to be the exclusive province of the "Son of man." In a few sweeping words the Son asserted His *pre-existence:* "He that came down from heaven"; *transcendence:* "the Son of man which is in heaven"; *omnipresence:* "which *is in* heaven"; and *union with the Father:* "the Son of man." This fact is amplified by the fascinating consideration that Jesus drew His present statement from Proverbs 30:4. "Who hath ascended up into heaven, or descended? who hath gathered the wind in his fists? who hath bound the waters in a garment? who hath established all the ends of the earth? what is his name, and what is his son's name, if thou canst tell?"

The verse strikes at the heart of the Jewish problem, ancient and modern. Tradition had obscured the clear word from the Old Testament record, which confirmed that the Messiah would be God incarnate. The Christ rooted His preparatory word in the prophetic soil of the Old Covenant's affirmation that the Messiah was in fact the Son of God.

Having completed His introduction, Jesus moved to reveal, in the simplest possible terms, His present mission.

The Son *came down* (3:13)
To be *lifted up* (3:14)
In order for man to *enter in* (3:15)

Nicodemus was speechless as Jesus proceeded to answer his
"how?" by revealing not only the how of the new birth but a glorious succession addressing every side of the question.

> *How?* By believing on the Son (3:15)
> *Why?* Because "God so loved" (3:16a)
> *Who?* "Whosoever" (3:16b)
> *What?* "Should not perish, but have everlasting life" (3:16c)
> *Where?* In this present world; "God sent his Son into the
>   world . . . that the world through him might be saved"
>   (3:17)
> *When?* At this moment—"he that believeth on him is not con-
>   demned" (3:18a)

While these magnificent truths were cascading from the lips of
Jesus Christ, a phenomenon was developing that would certainly
have captivated the attention of Nicodemus. For everything Jesus
was saying was rising from the sub-structure of Passover ceremonialism.

THE LAMB: GOD'S UPLIFTED OFFERING

"And as Moses lifted up the serpent in the wilderness, even so
must the Son of man be lifted up: that whosoever believeth in him
should not perish, but have eternal life" (John 3:14-15).

It is intriguing that Jesus chose another event in the history of ancient Israel through which to demonstrate the Lamb's being lifted up
(Numbers 21:5-9). As Passover was not exactly like the other offerings, His lifting up would also bear wider ramifications. As we have
considered, the element of substitution was paramount in Passover
and, for that matter, all offerings of the Levitical system. The
believer's laying of hands on the lamb at once identified the offerer
with the offering. The lamb became one with the repentant sinner
and suffered the penalty due the supplicant.

The serpent illustration, however, opened another vista of truth
concerning the work of God's final Lamb. The focus was placed on

the aspect of life coming out of death. Ancient tradition had taught the Jews that the serpent-bitten Israelites lifted up their eyes not simply to Moses' serpent of brass but to God Himself, who was extending mercy to those who would look to Him. Thus those who were doomed to death found life instead. It was no less than a picture of resurrection from death into a new life provided by God. Later Jewish tradition would magnify this by applying the symbol directly to the fact that the dead would live again. "Behold, if God made it that, through the similitude of the serpent that brought death, the dying should be restored to life, how much more shall He, Who is life, restore the dead to life."

It is as though the Lord fused the central aspects of Passover with the Feast of Firstfruits. The blood shed and applied would serve to guarantee resurrection—life would come out of death.

Jesus drew Nicodemus a verbal portrait of the historical event His hearer's eyes were later to behold. He spoke of the Lamb of God's being "lifted up" as the serpent in bygone days had been "lifted up." This lifting up was done so that whoever looked by faith would live. And so Nicodemus was led to the center pole of the New Covenant, not now set in the intricacies of Levitical ceremonialism but forever hereafter grounded in the fact that eternal life would be found through the "look" of faith to the Lamb of God, who was made sin for us. "For he hath made him to be sin for us, who knew no sin; that we might be made the righteousness of God in him" (2 Corinthians 5:21).

THE LAMB: GOD'S BURNT OFFERING

"For God so loved the world, that he gave his only begotten Son, that whosoever believeth in him should not perish, but have everlasting life" (John 3:16).

John 3:16 is the shimmering antitype of Israel's burnt offering. Nicodemus witnessed daily during Passover people coming to present their burnt offerings. These, as we have learned, were voluntary offerings expressing affection for and total surrender to God. The privileged Pharisee would hear the God-Man declare the supreme act of surrender—"God so loved the world, that he gave his only begotten Son. . ."

One wonders if the mind of Nicodemus was once again racing

with the astonished exclamation: "How can these things be?" Nearly two thousand years removed from the occasion, we feel prone to join him. It beggars comprehension, but there it stands. Every lamb, brought by every offerer, to every Jewish altar as a burnt offering, over every generation, pointed the way to the last Burnt Offering; one that was volunteered, not from a sense of duty or even pity, but because "God so loved."

THE LAMB: GOD'S PEACE OFFERING

"For God sent not his Son into the world to condemn the world, but that the world through him might be saved" (John 3:17).

Jesus' guest was well aware of the meaning of the peace offering—justification, acceptance, and peace with God. God's Son, Jesus explained, had come into the world to secure peace and bring salvation. Another Pharisee would grasp the import of it and register the result.

The Son *made peace*—"And, having made peace through the blood of his cross, by him to reconcile all things unto himself" (Colossians 1:20).

The Son *is our peace*—"For he is our peace, who hath made both one, and hath broken down the middle wall of partition between us" (Ephesians 2:14).

The Son *proclaimed peace*—"And came and preached peace to you who were afar off, and to them that were nigh" (Ephesians 2:17).

Nicodemus was hearing what Paul would so wonderfully express. Lasting—everlasting—peace and security had come in the person of Jesus, the Messiah. "Therefore, being justified by faith, we have peace with God through our Lord Jesus Christ, by whom also we have access by faith into this grace wherein we stand, and rejoice in hope of the glory of God" (Romans 5:1-2).

THE LAMB: OUR SOURCE OF REJOICING

Peace offerings—the final sacrifices of the festive season—were brought with rejoicing springing from the realization of what had been transacted through God's gracious provision. Jesus rounds out the revelation to Nicodemus by sounding the compatible fulfilling note that would reverberate across the face of the earth, resound throughout successive generations, and swell to fill the expanse of the eternity of God: "He that believeth on him is not condemned" (John 3:18*a*).

The melodic refrain is once again seized upon by Nicodemus's Pharisee contemporary Paul. "There is therefore now no condemnation to them which are in Christ Jesus" (Romans 8:1). It rings among us still through spoken testimony and hymnwriter's phrase,

> Now are we free—there's no condemnation,
> Jesus provides a perfect salvation.
> (Philip P. Bliss, "Once for All")

And what must it have meant to the man who was so earnestly seeking truth, a man who had given his life over to types, symbols, and ceremonies, hoping—ever hoping—only hoping that somehow he would find assurance of salvation and eternal peace before an offended God. As he excused himself and retreated through the streets of the night-shrouded city, the words must have sounded in his mind like the threefold blasts from the Temple trumpets: no condemnation; no condemnation; *no condemnation.*

For Nicodemus this had been a night truly different from all other nights. He had heard wondrous things.

What we have just seen is a magnificent example of the competence of Scripture in the communication of God's truth. Millions across the centuries have been led to this passage for exposure to what we view as the simplest declaration of God's reconciling grace set forth by the divine hand. Through its compelling words, multitudes from among those millions have come away with this Savior-love triumphant in their lives. Yet the same text, to which we bring our children, set before one whose life was wholly occupied with the complexities of the Levitical system, contained such a wealth of declarative, comparative, and illustrative material that the Holy Spirit had enough fuel for the fires of conviction to consume the mind and spirit of Nicodemus until he yielded to Israel's Messiah.

A LOOK BACK

Before we leave the scene of the first public Passover in our Savior's ministry, we should pause for a moment to look back at what Jesus said and did at that great feast. Briefly stated, He:

Asserted His authority (2:14-17)
Articulated the central evidence of the gospel (2:18-22)
Displayed His divine power (2:23)
Declared the new birth as a necessity (3:1-13)
Showed the Lamb as the uplifted offering (3:14-15)
Showed the Lamb as the burnt offering (3:16)
Showed the Lamb as the peace offering (3:17)
Showed the Lamb as the source of rejoicing (3:18)
Delineated the issues that must be settled (3:18-21)

All was done within the context of the Feast of Passover.

3
Sound the Trumpets

John 5:1-47

Trumpets called all Israel
    To solemn "awesome days."
Fears of judgment, death and woe
    Stalked their clouded ways.

The Father sent Him forth as Judge
    To end the bitter strife.
Offers resurrection sure—
    Jesus is the LIFE.

B ezetha was alive with the vigor of a young community. The suburb was pushing its way northward as markets, bazaars, and the shops of busy craftsmen drew from the city people who were in need of its products or skills. Children shouted to their friends as they ran about, dodging between plodding beasts and impatient Jerusalemites intent on completing their rounds. This little community, pressed hard against the northern wall of the Temple enclosure, was always a busy place.

Today, however, business endeavors gave way to religious activity, which was intensified by the influx of the thousands who were in the Holy City for another of Israel's festive seasons. Pilgrims walked through streets in the shadows of the brooding towers of the Antonia as they moved toward the gates leading to the sanctuary. On other days people might pause at the sheep market to purchase lambs for their offerings at the Temple. It would not be done on this day—it was the Sabbath. Something about the area was suggestively emblematic. The fortress, with its watchful occupants ever visible to the Jewish people entering the suburb, stood as a symbol of Roman oppression. But as legionnaires watched and listened, while pilgrims hurried past their conquerors' citadel, sounds heralding Israel's ultimate triumph in the Messiah rose about them—the bleating of sacrificial lambs.

To some, who were not religiously inclined, this was just another day in Jerusalem, a day warmed by the sun of early autumn and solemnized for the ceremonies of a Sabbath. But today it would be different. Bezetha would be warmed by another Sun, one that would set a glow over the place that could never be extinguished.

Jesus entered Bezetha unnoticed and unattended. He had come to Jerusalem alone. As He moved quietly along, His attention was not drawn to the Antonia, the sheepmarket, or the great entry gates into the Temple. Deliberately He directed His steps to a place of refuse, not a receptacle for the castoffs of people but a place of people who were cast off—human debris. As he reached His destination He saw spread before Him a shabby array of physical hulks who had fallen prey to malicious diseases—diseases that had dragged them to the point of no return. It was Jerusalem's repository for hopeless cases. Sightless eyes turned upward imploringly, as crippled limbs and twisted bodies cowered before their conquering infirmities. Babbling sounds came off inarticulate tongues attempting to frame expressions that would not take coherent dimensions in stunted minds. It was a place where maladies varied, but every heart and mind was fixed upon one thing—they were all waiting for a miracle.

Bethesda was a pool around which five porches had been arranged. On these porches, beside the pool, the infirm situated themselves and tarried, "waiting for the moving of the water. For an angel went down at a certain season into the pool, and troubled the water: whosoever then first after the troubling of the water stepped in was made whole of whatsoever disease he had" (5:3-4).

But for one who awaited troubled waters, a solution would be found in the presence of the Man who was accustomed to stilling them. "Wilt thou be made whole?" (5:6). This stranger, who from His appearance was obviously a Galilean, was asking something that scarcely required a reply. Was He mocking the old man who had already known more than full measure of ridicule? The head on the tattered mat turned for a look at the One who posed the apparently ludicrous question. Jesus' face answered his internal query, and the paralytic found himself saying, "Sir, I have no man, when the water is troubled, to put me into the pool: but while I am coming, another steppeth down before me" (5:7). It was a lament the man had raised many times in the wearying search for someone who cared enough to help him obtain his long-sought miracle.

Jesus' words were few but infused with revitalizing power. "Rise, take up thy bed, and walk" (5:8). The result was immediate and electrifying. His subject sprang to this feet, trembling with joy. As he did, a crowd quickly milled around this one they had known for such a long time. Their old companion in suffering was erect before them. His laments had turned to laughter, his pleas were transformed to praises, his lameness had given way to leaping. Had such a thing ever happened in all of Israel before? It had, indeed, and it would again. Jerusalem would see "greater works than this." By the time the man had gained his wits and sought out his mysterious benefactor, He was nowhere to be found. Jesus had quietly left the pool to continue His walk to the Temple, there to await the unfolding of the second phase of this astonishing transaction.

For his part, the man obeyed Jesus' instructions implicitly—he took up his bed and walked. One can imagine this thankful recipient of Jehovah's mercy hurrying away from the pool toward the massive gates leading to the sanctuary, where he would convey the news of his great good fortune to the priests and throngs of Sabbath worshipers. His euphoric enthusiasm was short-circuited, however, when instead of hosannas, he was accosted by cries of outrage. "It is the sabbath day; it is not lawful for thee to carry thy bed" (5:10). He for whom God had miraculously set aside physical laws in order to bring deliverance from suffering, now found himself being flogged by the inflexible strictures of human traditions. Religious enforcers gathered about with shaking fingers and crude catcalls of condemnatory derision. Befuddled, the man, so quickly robbed of his joy by men who judged themselves more pious than he, attempted to raise a defense. "He that made me whole, the same said unto me, Take up thy bed, and walk" (5:11).

We can be assured that there were lurking suspicions in the minds of his questioners when they asked, "What man is that which said unto thee, Take up thy bed, and walk?" (5:12). *Jesus of Nazareth,* they thought, *must be somewhere about.* It was like Him to despise God's Sabbath!

To their disappointment, the man could not name his benefactor—

a fact that was singularly important to the purpose of the Messiah, who at that moment may have observed the proceedings. The focus of attention was to be, for the moment, on the man and the miracle. Thus with careful intent Jesus had chosen a man who had lain prostrate before Israel's leadership for nearly four decades. His was a face that was all too familiar among frequenters of the Temple mount. He now stood before them completely whole, as if being forced to the center of the Temple stage for all to see.

It may have been a somewhat dejected figure, now left alone by his interrogators, who wandered across the gleaming stones of the Temple courts. Perhaps it was a hand on his shoulder that turned him about expecting once more to be questioned, or condemned. But no, he was again looking into the face of the author of the uproar, his beneficent Galilean. Before the man could blurt out his thanks, Jesus was speaking. "Behold, thou art made whole: sin no more, lest a worse thing come unto thee" (5:14).

We are not told whether Jesus instructed the man to go to the leadership of the Temple and identify Him as the one who had performed the miracle or not. The fact is, the man did so immediately, and the authorities reacted inflamed with the intent to kill.

There is no question that Jesus' act was purposely designed to provoke a confrontation with Jewry's Temple leadership—He had something to say to the nation. We have witnessed the point of *provocation;* now we shall examine the *occasion* and the Messiah's *explanation.*

THE OCCASION

"After this there was a feast of the Jews, and Jesus went up to Jerusalem" (5:1).

The feast chosen by God for a central declaration concerning His Son has been termed by some "the Unknown Feast." On the contrary, although it may properly be designated as an unnamed feast, it can hardly remain unknown to us, particularly in view of the contextual, ceremonial, and Temple Scripture readings available for examination.

Attempts by scholars to identify John's unnamed feast seem almost as varied as the sources consulted. Pentecost, Passover, Dedication, Purim, and Rosh Hashanah, and even an obscure occasion, "The Feast of the Wood-Offering," have all been set forth as possible contenders. In consulting authorities, however, one discovers an almost universal disregard for contextual clues contained in what Jesus did and said at this feast. We firmly believe that His conduct and discourse serve not only to identify the occasion but stand as an irrefutable link between the shadow of the festal ceremonialism and the substance of the revealed God-Man. Thus, we will not attempt to detail objections and postulates favoring or discounting other feasts but will simply harmonize the textual record with the historical and ceremonial events into which Jesus thrust Himself.

SOUND THE TRUMPETS

The period in question was, we are convinced, Rosh Hashanah, the Jewish feast of the New Year. This celebration was to be marked by a day-long blowing of silver trumpets and shofroth (rams' horns) in the ears of the nation. The feast is introduced in Leviticus:

> And the Lord spake unto Moses, saying, Speak unto the children of Israel, saying, In the seventh month, in the first day of the month, shall ye have a sabbath, a memorial of blowing of trumpets, an holy convocation. Ye shall do no servile work therein: but ye shall offer an offering made by fire unto the Lord. (Leviticus 23:23-25)

Trumpets, historically and typically, signify Israel's national return to the land of their fathers. But most significant, the emphasis is placed upon the regathering in preparation for Israel's embracing of her Messiah. Isaiah states the case clearly:

> And it shall come to pass in that day, that the Lord shall beat off from the channel of the river unto the stream of Egypt, and ye shall be gathered one by one, O ye children of Israel. And it shall come to pass in that day, that the great trumpet shall be blown, and they shall come which were ready to perish in the land of Assyria, and the outcasts in the land of Egypt, and they shall worship the Lord in the holy mount at Jerusalem. (Isaiah 27:12-13)

In this connection, Isaiah emphasizes the trumpets in their association with the lifting up of an ensign (18:3). The "ensign" is identified as the delivering Messiah in 11:10. "And in that day there shall be a root of Jesse, which shall stand for an ensign of the people; to him shall the Gentiles seek: and his rest shall be glorious."

There is an account of the observance of Rosh Hashanah in the book of Nehemiah (8:1-12), following Judah's wearying sojourn in Babylon. The remnant that had returned to Israel assembled on the "first day of the seventh month" (Tishri). As Ezra the scribe read the Torah (Moses) to the sons of Jacob, "all the people wept, when they heard the words of the Law." Trumpets was for them a day of national repentance that was turned to rejoicing and celebration.

Perhaps the most sweeping portrayal of the ramifications of the Feast of Trumpets is found in the book of Joel (2:1—3:21). "Blow the trumpet in Zion, sanctify a fast, call a solemn assembly" (2:15). Israel, the prophet tells us, is moving toward her greatest day of re-gathering. In his projection, he frames:

A call to repentance (2:1-14)
A question of Messiah (2:15-17)
A call to the nation (2:18—3:1)
A call to the nations (3:2-11)
A call to judgment (Gentile nations) (3:12-15)
A call from the Messiah (3:16)
A consummation under Messiah's reign (3:17-21)

With this we are treated to a magnificent foreview from the prepa-ratory regathering (Trumpets) to Israel's final reconciliation (Day of Atonement) and onward to her fulfilling ingathering (Tabernacles) under the sovereign sway of the reigning Messiah.

With these considerations in mind, let us return to the courts of the Temple and listen with Jesus to the sounding of the trumpets.

A DAY AMONG DAYS

As was the case with Passover, Rosh Hashanah marked the begin-ning of a festive season. It was Israel's second celebration of the New Year. Whereas Passover initiated the beginning of the religious year, Rosh Hashanah instituted the observance of the civil year. It also marked the beginning of the seventh (sabbatic) month of the year. This was a day of extreme importance in the national life of the Jewish people. When the silver trumpets and rams' horns were blown at the Temple, a period of worship began that covered twenty-two days.

Tishri (September/October)

1	Rosh Hashanah
2	
3	Awesome Days (Days of Penitence)
4	"
5	"
6	"
7	"
8	"
9	"
10	Yom Kippur (Day of Atonement)
11	
12	
13	
14	
15	Tabernacles
16	"
17	"
18	"
19	"
20	"
21	"
22	Holy Convocation (Sabbath)

THE NEW MOON

Israel's calendar year operated according to lunar reckoning. Therefore, a month's beginning was determined by the rising of the new moon. Each new moon's rise was an important event in Israel. Tishri's moon, however, was a very special event. It was, as we have observed, the beginning of the civil year. Beyond this, it was the seventh month, which was the sabbatical month of the year. Also, it ushered in the most serious period of religious contemplation for the people of the Book. So Tishri's moon heralded "the New Year for years, the New Year par excellence."

Exact timing for the rising of the new moon was established through an intricate system devised to insure accuracy. Eyewitnesses were essential to the process. Not one, but at least two or more were required to properly certify the event. To accommodate the process, the Sanhedrin sat in official session in the Hall of Hewn Stones at the Temple to receive and examine witnesses. In the event cloud cover obscured the heavens to Jerusalemites, injunctions against Sabbath travel were suspended to allow witnesses to convey the news as rapidly as possible. When witnesses had been properly examined and the council's solemn deliberations completed, a proclamation was issued, "It is sanctified," and the feast commenced. Trumpets and shofar were blown the day long. It is of interest to find that the use of horns from calves was forbidden, lest God be reminded of Israel's sin with the golden calf. Rams' horns were preferred because they memorialized Isaac's sacrificial encounter at Moriah long years before. On this year, the horns would herald the arrival of Jehovah's antitypical Isaac.

Jews of the Diaspora would learn of the new moon's appearance by way of a series of signal fires lighted on hilltops. These fires sent the news to those who lived in the hinterlands. The witnesses had seen, the Council had declared, the trumpets had sounded—let the celebration begin!

Following the proclamation by the Sanhedrin, the eyewitnesses were honored in a banquet hall, Beth Yaazek, especially designed for the purpose, and Israel's credible witnesses became temporary celebrities.

AWESOME DAYS

Rosh Hashanah was not, however, a time primarily given to great gaiety. It was a time characterized by hushed solemnity as the nation came to grips with the reality of sin and their inevitable appointment before the divine Judge. It was believed by the Jews of the period that Rosh Hashanah was the day when God judged mankind. They believed "the judgment commenced immediately after the Jewish Sanhedrin had settled that the new moon of Tishri had actually risen." Any aspect of rejoicing was in anticipation of Jehovah's mercy's being extended to penitents.

Another dominant theme of Rosh Hashanah emphasized the recognition of Jehovah as King over His people. Ancient rabbinical sources confirm "the theme of God as King is particularly stressed on Rosh Hashanah, because of the day's association with His judgment."

"Three books are opened on Rosh Hashanah, one for the completely righteous, one for the completely wicked, and one for average persons. The completely righteous are immediately inscribed in the book of life. The completely wicked are immediately inscribed in the book of death. The average persons are kept in suspension from Rosh Hashanah to the Day of Atonement. If they deserved well, they are inscribed in the book of life, if they do not deserve well, they are inscribed in the book of death.'' Having one's name written in the book of life carried temporal as well as eternal connotations. "A good life in a good year" was the thought.

Rabbinical explanations as to why trumpets were blown on this day are reasoned to be tenfold. We quote several that are of interest:

"Trumpets are sounded at a coronation and God is hailed as king on this day.

The shofar heralds the beginning of the penitential season. (From Rosh Hashanah to the Day of Atonement.)

The ram was substituted for Isaac.

The prophet Zephaniah speaks of the great 'day of the Lord' (Judgment Day) as a day of the horn of alarm (Zephaniah 1:14-16).

The prophet Isaiah speaks of the great shofar which will herald the messianic age (Isaiah 27:13).

The shofar will be sounded at the resurrection" (cited by Louis Jacobs quoting Saadiah Gaon [ancient source] in *Judaica,* vol. 14, p. 308).

Some have raised questions as to whether these thoughts all pertained in the days of our Lord's sojourn on this planet. Whatever may or may not be argued on the subject, we can be certain that the people in Jerusalem, when Jesus arrived at the feast, were taken up with prevailing thoughts of *judgment, life, death,* and *resurrection.* Consistent with this observation is the ancient portrayal of Jehovah as standing before the nation as Judge with a scale extended before the nation, which was being "weighed in the balances." Another commentator says it was customary at this season for some elderly Jews to wear death shrouds as they walked the streets in graphic demonstration of the solemnities of the season. So the "Ten Awesome Days" observed during Israel's approach to her high holy Day of Atonement were not ones of hilarity and celebration but rather ones of quiet trepidation and subdued festivity in anticipation of God's mercy.

READINGS IN THE TEMPLE

Readers of the New Testament will find that the Scriptures were read regularly in the synagogues and at the Temple worship services. Acts 15:21 states, "For Moses [from generations of old] hath in every city them that preach him, being read in the synagogues every Sabbath.'' Indeed, when Jesus preached in the synagogue at Nazareth, He was handed a scroll containing the writings of Isaiah (Luke 4:17), which suggests not only regular readings from the Torah (Pentateuch), but the prophets as well. Having said this, the question immediately arises as to what system was followed in the arrangement of selections from the Torah and haphtarah (the lesson from the prophets, which amplified the reading from Moses).

Aileen Guilding, in *The Fourth Gospel and Jewish Worship* (Oxford Press, 1960) has, in conjunction with the work of Audolph Büchler, conducted exhaustive research on this subject. They have agreed on a triennial system of readings based on the lunar calendar, which would accomplish the public reading of the Pentateuch over a three-year cycle. The attendant haphtarah readings from the prophets covered a corresponding period. The cycle of readings arrived at by this system has an obvious and very logical association with the discourses of Jesus at the Temple and in the synagogues. We are, through these Old Testament Scriptures, afforded an illuminating glimpse of what the priests and people had before them at the time, as well as a magnificent view of the living Word in climactic interaction with the written Word of God.

THE WORD

Among the Temple readings for New Year's day one finds Leviticus 4, a portion that speaks of sin, sacrifice, and forgiveness. Also found are words from Ezekiel 18:30, "Therefore, I will judge you, O house of Israel, every one according to his ways, saith the Lord God. Repent, and turn yourselves from all your transgressions; so iniquity shall not be your ruin." A reading from Deuteronomy brings home the theme of judgment. "Ye shall not respect persons in judgment, but ye shall hear the small as well as the great; ye shall not be afraid of the face of man, for the judgment is God's" (Deuteronomy 1:17).

Dr. Büchler also cites Joel 2 as a haphtarah reading for the New Year. "Blow ye the trumpet in Zion, and sound an alarm in my holy mountain: Let all the inhabitants of the land tremble: for the day of the Lord cometh, for it is nigh at hand. . . . Therefore also now, saith the Lord, turn ye to me with all your heart, and with fasting, and with weeping, and with mourning: and rend your heart, and not your garments, and turn unto the Lord your God: for he is gracious and merciful, slow to anger, and of great kindness" (Joel 2:1, 12-13).

Running through these selections is also the theme of the revelation of God. Genesis 28, which records Jacob's night dream of the ladder extending to heaven, says, "And, behold, the Lord stood above it, and said, I am the Lord God of Abraham, thy father, and the God of Isaac" (28:13). Another notable example is the seasonal reading from Exodus, which records Moses' encounter with deity. "The Lord spake unto Moses face to face, as a man speaketh unto his friend" (Exodus 33:11).

THE WORKER

The air of the Temple courts carried the resounding proclamations of the One who looked into the livid countenances of those who were prepared to stone Him. Their sensitivities, already wounded by His apparent disregard for the Sabbath, were cut deeper still by His words. "My Father worketh hitherto, and I work" (5:17). Menacing gestures and ominous murmurings made it only too clear that His opponents understood precisely what Jesus was proposing. He said "that God was his Father, making himself equal with God" (5:18). They were correct. He had claimed to be at one with the Father and in so doing set three great towers of truth in place.

1. The Messiah's Godhood
    "My Father worketh hitherto, and I work" (5:17). In this statement He claimed *oneness with Jehovah.* "For the Father loveth the Son, and showeth him all things that himself doeth; and he will show him greater works than these" (5:20). The implication here is clearly one of *co-regency* between Jesus and the Father. In other words, the Temple hierarchy stood in the presence of their *King.* "That all men should honor the Son, even as they honor the Father" (5:23). The God-King is *worthy to receive worship.*

2. The Messiah's judgeship
    "For the Father judgeth no man, but hath committed all judgment unto the Son" (5:22). The recording Spirit is very careful to press the *scope* and *significance* of Jesus as universal Judge. Its *scope* was all inclusive: "But hath committed *all* judgment unto the Son" (5:22). Its *significance* was all surpas-

sing: "The resurrection of life . . . the resurrection of damnation" (5:29).

3. The Messiah as lifegiver

The revelatory sequence is bent toward a consuming purpose. "For as the Father raiseth up the dead, and [giveth them life], even so the Son [giveth life] to whom he will" (5:21). A consummating declaration is laid before the Temple audience: Jesus of Nazareth is the *dispenser of life*. And as His hearers pondered the proportions of that word, He quickly constructed a succession of clarifying statements.

THE PROCESS OF PASSAGE

"Verily, verily, I say unto you, He that heareth my word, and believeth on him that sent me, hath everlasting life, and shall not come into condemnation, but is passed from death unto life" (5:24).

Notice how emphatically Israel's Messiah sets forth the necessity of conjunctive faith—a fusion of trust in the speaking Son and the sending Father. They must "honor the Son, even as they honor the Father" (5:23). Beyond this, it is not restricted to a functional exercise in worship, honoring the Son, but a foundational concept showing how men come to grasp life from God. The Son must be received as the *messenger of life,* but at one and the same time He is the *divine essence of life.* "For as the Father hath life in himself, so hath he given to the Son to have life in himself" (5:26).

Oneness with the Father is achieved through union with the Son.

A PRESENT POSSESSION

"Verily, verily, I say unto you, The hour is coming, and now is, when the dead shall hear the voice of the Son of God; and they that hear shall live" (5:25).

Men came up to Jerusalem during this solemn season seeking a measure of assurance for the future. What they heard swept beyond their grandest spiritual expectations. Jesus was telling them that "the hour now is" when men who are estranged from God can lay hold on eternal life. It is salvation in the here-and-now with the assurance that they need never fear "coming into judgment," having "passed from death to life."

Ears were hearing an aspect of the gospel of grace that had only been seen through the mists of prophecy, ceremony, and typology.

Now it was being exposed to them in the person and power of Jesus Christ. He had come to put man's fear of death and judgment to rest. He was life, and those who rested in Him could possess His life at this moment.

THE PERMANENT CONSEQUENCES

"Marvel not at this: for the hour is coming, in the which all that are in the graves shall hear his voice, and shall come forth; they that have done good, unto the resurrection of life; and they that have done evil, unto the resurrection of damnation" (5:28-29).

Having proclaimed the good, the only way to life, He outlined the alternatives in prospect as a result of their decision. Those consequences were personal and eternal. Every son of Adam will one day "hear his voice," shake off the dust of the sepulcher, and quit his tomb. Bodily resurrection is a certainty. Every man will receive his eternal due according to his present choice.

At Passover, it was a Pharisee, Nicodemus, who had heard words from the Messiah that caused him to wonder, "How can these things be?" It was now time for the Sadducees to call a caucus. Jesus had deliberately and decisively devastated one of their most fondly held fallacies. There was, He informed them, a resurrection in their future. Sadducean sensibilities were bruised by blows from two directions. First, He had declared them to be in error about the most basic question relating to man's eternal destiny. Additionally, in presenting His physical resurrection, Jesus was agreeing with their persistent theological antagonists, the Pharisees.

THE SADDUCEES

The sect of the Sadducees provides a rather interesting paradox. On the one hand, they are seen as hellenized, urbane, and worldly. These Sadducees, however, are also viewed as inflexible, letter-of-the-word people who saw their Pharisaic contemporaries as those who had diverted their steps from the path of true religion. They sincerely regarded themselves as the stalwart guardians of Jehovah's truth.

In order to come to a relatively accurate assessment of the Sadducees, it is helpful to view the group from *external* and *internal* perspectives.

External considerations were linked to Sadducean status in the affairs of the nation. Their ranks were composed of the wealthier elements in Jewry. Priests, merchants, and members of the aristocrasy composed the small but understandably influential party. Sadducees, consequently, were the people who dealt more directly with the emmissaries of Rome. They shared a vested interest in the preservation of peace with their overlords and, as a result, were quite prepared to adopt a posture of acquiescence toward the governing authorities.

One source accurately records the Sadducean approach: "The primary concern of the Sadducees in all of this was to keep the nation peaceable and thereby to avoid trouble for the Romans and, in turn, themselves" (D. A. Hagner, *Zondervan Pictorial Bible Dictionary,* vol. 5, p. 213). This was, of course, seen as appeasement by the common people, who rewarded the Sadducees with increasing measures of contempt. Because of this situation, some have projected the sect as a compromising, politically motivated faction.

The Sadducees' station, religiously, however, turns the coin to the internal side of things and presents another picture. The priestly Temple leadership, as we have noted, was predominantly made up of Sadducees. And although at this period Rome was beginning to play musical chairs with the high priest's position, imperial selections were consistently drawn from among the ruling families of Sadducees.

Sadducees saw themselves as inflexible conservatives. They were men of the letter. In the conduct of rituals and making decisions regarding judgments and penalties they were noted for their unswerving severity. They also rejected pharisaic belief in the oral law. Sadducees accepted only the Scriptures as authoritative. Some go so far as to say they were willing to accept only the writings of Moses as fully inspired. That probably was not the case, but it may be safe to say that they majored in Moses and minored in Israel's writing prophets. "In their reactionary conservativism the Sadducees attempted to capitalize on their self-made image of themselves as protectors of the pure and true religion which alone *went back to Moses*" (Hagner, *ZPBD,* vol. 5, p. 215).

Their brand of professed biblicism, however, produced some concepts far removed from what was taught by Moses or the prophets. We note a few:

1. Sadducees held that there was no bodily resurrection, future life, bliss, or rewards.

2. Angels and demons did not exist.
3. Man's free will was absolute. He alone was the author of his bliss or misery, which was, of course, enjoyed or endured in this world.

The conflict between the Sadducees and Pharisees has been termed "a struggle between two concepts of God. The Sadducees sought to bring God down to man. Their God was anthropomorphic and the worship offered him was like homage paid to a human king or ruler. The Pharisees on the other hand, sought to raise man to divine heights and to bring him nearer to a spiritual and transcendent God" (cited by J. Z. Lauterbach in *Judaica*, vol. 14, p. 621).

THE WITNESSES

It had been perhaps but a matter of hours since the spokesman for the Sanhedrin had risen to declare, "It is sanctified." Eyewitnesses to the rising of Tishri's new moon had been declared trustworthy and the testimony officially certified. They were judged Israel's credible witnesses to an indispensible element of national life— nothing could move forward until the witnesses spoke and the leadership examined, believed, and announced the event.

The God-Man would now bring His eyewitnesses forward to be presented before Israel's ruling body. Meticulously, He had chosen the moment in order to bring the event into the sharpest possible focus. Jesus had made majestic declarations, declarations that only God could make. Boldly, He summoned four witnesses to testify that the prophet Malachi's parting word to a fading dispensation was today fulfilled. The morning had arrived. The Sun of righteousness had risen with healing in His wings (Malachi 4:2).

Jesus' opening statement has troubled a few people. "If I bear witness of myself, my witness is not true" (John 5:31). He was not, of course, proposing that He was less than a credible witness. One need only remember the requirements for official validation of testimony in Israel. A single witness was not sufficient, true though his words might be, to establish judicial credibility. Our Lord was simply saying that, in this sense, they would not receive His witness.

THE FIRST WITNESS: JOHN THE BAPTIST (5:32-35)

"Ye sent unto John, and he bare witness unto the truth" (5:33). Not only had they heard and examined the Baptist, but "were willing for a season to rejoice in his light" (5:35).

What witness had John borne before them?

The primacy of messianic prophetic Scriptures (1:19-27). John's annunciation identified his mission as the footman of the promised Messiah, using Isaiah 40 as one of his proof texts.

A visual confirmation (1:32-33). "And John bare record, saying, I saw the Spirit descending from heaven like a dove, and it abode upon him" (1:33).

An affirmation of Jesus' deity (1:34). "And I saw and bare record that this is the Son of God." John made it clear that, as the Messiah's forerunner, he was preparing "a highway for our God" (Isaiah 40:3).

THE SECOND WITNESS: HIS WORKS (5:36)

At Nazareth, in the synagogue, He had read from the prophet Isaiah. "The Spirit of the Lord is upon me, because he hath anointed me to preach the gospel to the poor; he hath sent me to heal the brokenhearted, to preach deliverance to the captives, and recovering of sight to the blind, to set at liberty them that are bruised" (Luke 4:18). Standing among them at the Temple that day were some former "captives" who had been set at "liberty." We believe the man who had laid beside Bethesda's pool stood close at hand. Who could argue with this "work" of Christ? There were certainly enough people present who could testify as eyewitnesses to his prolonged suffering. A lengthy procession could have been called to raise a finger of identification and say, "Yes, this is the man. The one who lay at our feet imploring, now stands at our side rejoicing!" Sadducees, Pharisees, and worshipers had but to look about them not only to see his but other faces dotting the crowd as living testimonials to Jesus' power to deliver.

THE THIRD WITNESS: THE FATHER'S WORD (5:37-38)

At Jesus' baptism, with emissaries from the Temple undoubtably in attendance, the Father had spoken from heaven. "And, lo, a voice from heaven saying, This is my beloved Son, in whom I am well pleased" (Matthew 3:17). Consider the fact that in certifying the rising of the new moon the Sanhedrin accepted first what the witnesses had *seen.* This was sealed in their minds by what they themselves had *heard*. Jesus' works were *seen*; the Father's words were *heard*. And the approbation from heaven was a direct reflection of another testimonial word from the Father. "Behold my servant, whom I uphold; mine elect, in whom my soul delighteth; I have put my Spirit upon him; he shall bring forth judgment to the Gentiles" (Isaiah 42:1).

But, alas, as with their hearts, so with their heads. "Ye have neither *heard* his voice, at any time, or *seen* his shape" (5:37). Further, they had not His word "abiding in them" (5:38), and refused to believe the one "whom he hath sent." With these fateful words, He detailed the depths of their spiritual destitution.

THE FOURTH WITNESS: THE SCRIPTURES (5:39-47)

His final witness would be the Scriptures and the one who was revered above all others by His hearers, Moses himself. The Son brushed aside their popular occupation with pursuing the sacred writings in quest of evidences of self-justification, condemnation of their adversaries, or the glorification of their parties. Of the Word which they professed to believe with their whole hearts, He said, "They are they which testify of me" (5:39). His was an appeal to search Scriptures in the true earnestness of men who sought light and life. Failure to do so would insure the sounding in the courtroom of the divine Judge another accusing voice. Moses would rise as the prosecuting attorney, who would articulate the proportions of their flagrant disregard of the Word of God. "For had ye believed Moses, ye would have believed me; for he wrote of me" (5:46).

A trumpet had sounded in Zion. Now the trumpeter would leave them and return to the green vales of Galilee. The notes had penetrated to the point of palsying the hands dedicated to His destruction, and His opponents parted before Him like a gentle wave as He left the Temple. It was only a temporary lull.

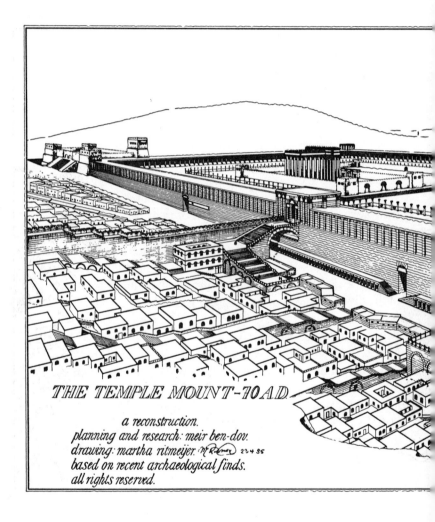

THE TEMPLE MOUNT - 70 A.D.

a reconstruction.
planning and research: meir ben-dov.
drawing: martha ritmeijer. 22-4-85
based on recent archaeological finds.
all rights reserved.

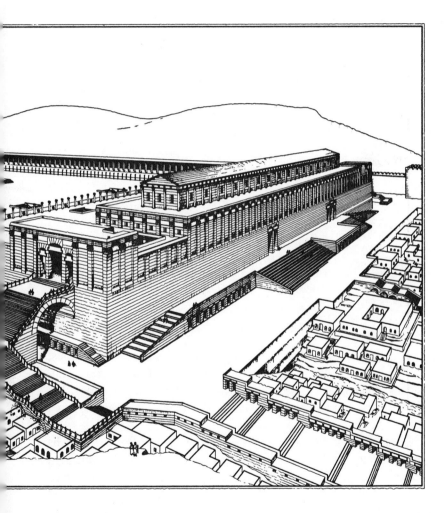

4
Manna for Mankind

John 6:1-71

Multitudes enraptured sat
 To hear all Christ had spoken,
Then he fed them, every one,
 With loaves His hands had broken.

"Come now, feed your hungry souls.
 Partake of Me," He said.
Heaven's Manna yours to eat—
 Jesus is the BREAD.

THE SECOND PASSOVER

A fuse was burning in Galilee, one that carried the ominous, hissing sound of an impending explosion of insurrection. Galileans, long noted for short tempers and passionate loyalties, believed their moment had finally arrived. Converging events spurred them on.

Jesus was the talk of every vale and village in the district. His months-long Galilean ministry had attracted massive attention among the people. Empowered disciples had gone in appointed pairs through the towns casting out demons, healing the sick, and preaching His gospel. In concert with this, one could hardly fail to notice the influx of Jerusalem-based religious authorities who watched, listened, questioned, and hurried away toward Judea with their reports. These brethren from the south, who had scarcely seemed to acknowledge the existence of Galilee in the past, now allowed nothing to go unnoticed. In the minds of His Temple critics, there was just cause for concern. As if their religious problems with the Galilean were not enough, they were deeply troubled over the prospect of trouble with Rome.

In this they were quite correct, for other eyes were worriedly fixed on Jesus and Galilee. The tetrarch Herod Antipas, incestuous and superstitious, had months before laid hands on John the Baptist and thrown him into prison at the Fortress Machaerus in southern Perea. Herod probably resided in Perea rather than Galilee during the period of Jesus' rising popularity. (Perea occupied a wedge of territory east of the Jordan between Samaria and the cities of Decapolis. It extended southward to a point where the Arnon River entered the Dead Sea.) John was liberated from the steamy dungeon by way of the executioner's sword following Salome's seductive dance and Herodias's (Salome's mother) infamous demand for John's head on a platter (Matthew 14:1-12).

At about the same time news of the Baptist's murder reached Jesus, Herod was receiving alarming reports of the Messiah's soaring popularity:

> Now Herod the tetrarch heard of all that was done by him: and he was perplexed, because that it was said of some, that John was risen from the dead; and of some, that Elijah had appeared; and by others, that one of the old prophets was risen again. And Herod said, John have I beheaded: but who is this, of whom I hear such things? And he desired to see him. (Luke 9:7-9)

The disciples, perhaps upon hearing of John's death, returned to His side to make their reports and await developments (Luke 9:10). At this time Jesus left Herod's jurisdiction and with His disciples crossed to the eastern side of the Jordan—where the river enters the Sea of Galilee from the north—to an area near Bethsaida-Julias, a city in the domain of the tetrarch Philip.

A shiver of excitement and anticipation ran through the hamlets rimming the lake. From squat, dark basalt-stone houses people filled the lanes and waterways to search out and hear what their rabbi would say and do. They gathered about Him in a "desert place," an expanse reposing lush and lovely beneath the temperate tutelage of spring. What a sight it must have been. Thousands of people spilling onto the plain from every direction. Sitting, standing, reclining in the field with upturned faces, He saw them there "and was moved with compassion toward them, because they were as sheep not having a shepherd" (Mark 6:34). These were *leaderless sheep*: The Baptist lay headless in his grave, while their spiritual counselors were failing them. They were *threatened sheep*: the wrath of a lusting, vengeful Herod clouded their future. They were *hungry sheep*, but in more ways than one the sheep would be fed that day.

"And the passover, a feast of the Jews, was nigh" (6:4).

John draws our attention to the central consideration. History, ceremony, and eternal reality were once again coming together. Passover season was upon them. As a matter of fact, many who listened to Jesus' words at Bethsaida may well have been pilgrims on the way to the feast at Jerusalem. The God-Man had selected the occasion to make His Passover address to the people. The emphasis rests there—*to the people*. One year hence, He would go up to Jerusalem and live out His grand Passover *for the people*. But this Passover, away from the haranguing opposition of priestly voices in the Holy City, would be uniquely His Passover address to the people.

PRELUDE (6:5-14)

Jesus was preparing to feed, with a boy's lunch, five thousand men, in addition to the women and children who were on the scene. His miracle of multiplication contains distinct divisions.

THE QUESTION (6:5)

"He saith unto Philip, Whence shall we buy bread, that these may eat?" His was a query designed to emphasize the lack of human resources. The question was rhetorical. It was not asked in order to receive an answer from Philip, "for he himself knew what he would do" (6:6). Already, His disciples had assessed the situation from their perspective. Comparing the Synoptic records with John's account, we are confronted by an impressive list of negatives:

1. *Not the right place*—"For we are here in a desert place" (Luke 9:12)

2. *Not enough bread*—"We have no more but five loaves and two fishes" (Luke 9:13)
3. *Not enough money*—Two hundred denarii (nearly a year's wages) "worth of bread is not sufficient" (John 6:7)
4. *Not enough manpower*—"Send the multitude away, that they may go into the villages, and *buy themselves [food]*" (Matthew 14:15, italics added)
5. *Not enough time*—The time is now late (Matthew 14:15)

The opinion was unanimous: Situation impossible; send them away.

THE PROVISION (6:9-13)

Jesus *took what they had* and provided a divine solution. It was the commonest of common fare. Barley loaves, the bread of the poor; little (sardinelike) fish, the meat of the poor; willow or wicker baskets, the vessels of the poor.

Having raised words of thanks, "he distributed to the disciples, and the disciples to them that were set down; and likewise of the fishes as much as they would. When they were filled, he said unto his disciples, Gather up the fragments that remain, that nothing be lost" (6:11-12). Twelve baskets brimming with loaves and fish were set before the Provider by beaming disciples. The people were fully satisifed. Every one had eaten all he wanted or required.

THE EXCLAMATION (6:14)

"Then those men, when they had seen the miracle that Jesus did, said, This is of a truth that prophet that should come into the world."

Gospel writers are of one accord in recording the fact that five thousand were present at this event. Matthew is even more specific than his peers in adding that the five thousand were "men, beside the women and children" (14:21). I am convinced that the Holy Spirit's purpose in this detail was not simply to inform us of Jesus' popularity. Nor do I believe it was primarily to manifest the magnitude of the miracle, although it certainly serves to accomplish this. I conclude rather that the emphasis on the numerical aspect is given to demonstrate the dimensions of the popular decision. The word translated "men" in the King James Version (John 6:14) should be rendered "people." Jesus of Nazareth was hailed as "the prophet" (the Messiah) by a host, even allowing for some dissenters, roughly equivalent to the numbers of registered Pharisees and Sadducees in all of Israel. They had the evidence—His miracle. It was theirs now but to crown their Messiah as sovereign and await His directives.

At this point many conclude their sermons. What a wonderful, tidy presentation—a perfect three-point message:

1. The People
2. The Provision
3. The Proclamation

It can be evangelistic, missionary, or a great motivator to personal evangelism. To finish here, however, is to bring an end where God is only beginning. The popular outcry raises the problem—it does not suggest that the solution had been found. And identifying the issue was precisely what Jehovah intended to do at this point. For the fact is that within a very short time it would be said of the vast majority of these people, "From that time many of his disciples went back, and walked no more with him" (6:66). And so the controversy was ignited. Some point to this passage and say, "You see, it is very clear—one can accept Christ and choose to disbelieve and become un-Christian again." Others counter by saying, "No, it is very clear that these people believed with a *head* knowledge but never possessed Christ in their *hearts.*" In other words, they were never true believers in the first place.

Who then is correct? Neither. And if there are a few points in this book where we need to erect the time-worn notice: STOP - LOOK - LISTEN! this is one of them. For in reality, they did believe in their heads and hearts that Jesus was Israel's true Messiah. This is not the issue. The fundamental question is posed in asking what they believed *about* the Messiah. Our problem is one of historical disorientation. That is, we approach the subject from a biblically revealed point of view—from what we have accepted, correctly, as biblical and Christian. But to impose our facts as preconceptions on the majority of those people is completely erroneous. It is of the utmost importance that we understand their problem, because it is basic to the question emphatically answered in the gospel of John.

RABBINICAL JUDAISM VERSES BIBLICAL JUDAISM

Most of Jesus' listeners that day believed the rabbinical teaching then current concerning the coming Messiah. A Jewish commentator explains their belief.

"The Messiah was expected to attain for Israel the idyllic blessings of the prophets; he was to defeat the enemies of Israel, restore the people to the Land, reconcile them to God, and introduce a period of spiritual and physical bliss. He was to be a prophet, warrior, judge, king, and teacher of Torah" (cited by Gerald J. Blidstein in *Judaica,* vol. 11, p. 1411). "However," another clarifies, "the Messiah was always the agent of God and never a savior in the Christian sense. The Davidic origin of the kingly messiah was supposed; but, as it seems, the messianic pretender had to prove his authenticity by his deeds" (cited by David Flusser in *Judaica,* vol. 11, p. 1410).

Alfred Edersheim, noted Hebrew-Christian historian, comments further. "First, the idea of a Divine Personality, and the union of the two natures in the Messiah, seems to have been foreign to the Jewish auditory [hearing] of Jesus of Nazareth and even at first to His disciples" (Alfred Edersheim, *Life and Times of Jesus the Messiah*). Popular rabbinic teaching in the time of Jesus portrayed the Messiah as a God-empowered man who was less than divine. The principal emphases were those of Messiah as a warrior-king. Thus the cry to force Jesus to the throne.

Edersheim continues: "Secondly, they appear to have regarded the Messiah as far above the ordinary human, royal, prophetic, and even Angelic type, to such an extent, that the boundary line separating it from the Divine Personality is of the narrowest, so that, when the conviction of the reality of the Messianic manifestation in Jesus burst on their minds, this boundary-line was easily, almost naturally overstepped, and those who would have shrunk from forming their belief in such dogmatic form readily owned and worshiped Him as the Son of God" (Edersheim, *Life and Times*).

Essentially, the people were faced with a transition from the obscurity of traditional rabbinical teaching to the clarity of the divine Messiah concept, which was the central theme of true biblical Judaism. In the clearest possible terms, people were called upon to make their decision about the Godhood of Jesus Christ. We can now understand that the miracle was simply a window through which those who had eaten would view and decide about that true Bread "come down from heaven."

THE PROPOSITION (6:22-59)

Jesus refused to accept homage as king and "departed again into a mountain himself alone" (6:15). He remained in seclusion while the disciples set out for Capernaum, coming to them later, walking on the turbulent waters that threatened to swamp their little boat (6:16-21). Following that eventful evening the people who had been miraculously satisfied with bread sought Him whom they had declared to be the promised one. "When the people therefore saw that Jesus was not there, neither his disciples, they also took boats and came to Capernaum, seeking for Jesus" (6:24). He was found in a picturesque fishing village.

Capernaum was nestled on the northwestern shore of Galilee, approximately two miles from where the Jordan enters the lake. The town lay on a gentle slope rising from one of the numerous shallow coves which lend a gracefully serpentine appearance to the shoreline. It was one of those places artists dream of discovering.

Beyond the fishing boats, shops, and houses stood a lovely synagogue. The structure was relatively new in the time of Christ, having recently been built by a benevolent Roman centurion. Their house of worship was constructed of white limestone, which was a marked contrast from the buildings surrounding it. Those were of dark, almost black, stone commonly used in the area. Visitors were properly impressed as they walked from the beach, where the odor of fish was heavy in the air, through the narrow streets until the imposing structure came into view. Townspeople must have taken great delight in watching faces of newcomers light up in wonderment at their first glimpse of their town's pride and joy.

Capernaum enjoyed some prominence in the region. The Romans thought it important enough to establish a customs house there. You will remember that Levi (Matthew) the publican collected taxes from it for a time. Roman troops were also garrisoned near the town—at least one hundred. A high-ranking government official apparently resided there, although we are not made aware of his functions. Numbered among the town's prominent people was Zebedee,

HERODIAN PALESTINE DURING CHRIST'S MINISTRY

whose sons, James and John, became disciples of Jesus. Peter also maintained a home there.

But above all else Capernaum had one special distinction—it was home and the center of ministry for Jesus after He departed Nazareth. Here, in addition to the miracles specifically mentioned in the gospels, He did many "mighty works." His presence brought Capernaum privileges far above those of her beauty, thriving economy, or provincial prominence. Unfortunately, theirs would be a privilege sorely abused. For the Messiah of Israel would declare of that proud city, "And thou, Capernaum, which art exalted unto heaven, shalt be brought down to hell: for if the mighty works, which have been done in thee, had been done in Sodom, it would have remained until this day" (Matthew 11:23). Capernaum's present condition bears eloquent testimonial to the weight of His condemnation.

Jesus walked up the street leading to the synagogue for the services of the Sabbath. It must have been slow going for Him and His band of disciples as they were pressed about by townspeople and the remnants of the multitude who had eaten to the full. Already they were shouting questions. His answers would be given in the synagogue.

"Rabbi, when camest thou here?" they asked. Jesus immediately responded by focusing attention on the eternal issues at hand. "Labor not for the meat which perisheth, but for that meat which endureth unto everlasting life" (6:27). "Then said they unto Him, What shall we do, that we might work the works of God?" (6:28). Next He stated the proposition. "Jesus answered and said unto them, This is the work of God, that *ye believe on him whom he hath sent*" (6:29, italics added).

A predictable question was raised asking for yet another sign to confirm His messiahship (6:30). "Our fathers did eat manna in the desert; as it is written, He gave them bread from heaven to eat" (6:31). This reference to the manna corresponds directly to what we are told would have been among synagogue readings for the season. Readings appropriate to Passover were taken from, among others, Exodus 16 and Numbers 11. Jesus' discourse is directly related to the subjects found in these texts and related Passover selections.

Some may wonder why unleavened bread was not the subject for His Passover declaration. It is an intriguing question. He was, of course, the "unleavened" (sinless) Bread of Life. But as all types and symbols have limitations, so it is in this case. There is a beautiful collaboration of types set before us by our Lord, which are given to expand and illuminate the entire subject. Christ, the Bread of Life, was not *born of haste*, as was true with Israel's bread of the Exodus. He was rather the Bread *sent from heaven* pictured in Israel's manna. "Verily, verily, I say unto you, Moses gave you not that bread from heaven; but my Father giveth you the true bread from heaven. For the bread of God is he which cometh down from heaven, and giveth life unto the world" (6:32-33).

A comparision—based on calculations of seasonal reading discussed in the previous chapter—of Passover Sabbath synagogue selections and Jesus' address demonstrates, once again, vital interaction between the written and living Word. It also projects the importance of the relationship between the feast and His announcement of deity. Additionally, it provides a vital picture of what was in the ears and minds of His hearers.

Isaiah 55:2
Wherefore do ye spend money for that which is not bread? And your labor for that which satisfieth not? Hearken diligently unto me, and eat that which is good, and let your soul delight itself in fatness.

John 6:27
Labor not for the meat which perisheth, but for that meat which endureth unto everlasting life, which the Son of man shall give unto you: for him hath God the Father sealed.

Isaiah 54:13
And all thy children shall be taught of the Lord, and great shall be the peace of thy children.

John 6:45
It is written in the prophets, And they shall all be taught of God. Every man therefore that hath heard, and hath learned of the Father, cometh unto me.

Numbers 11:13
Whence should I have flesh to give unto all this people? For they weep unto me, saying, Give us flesh, that we may eat.

John 6:51, 55
I am the living bread which came down from heaven: if any man eat of this bread, he shall live for ever; and the bread that I will give is

my flesh, which I will give for the life of the world. . . . For my
flesh is meat indeed, and my blood is drink indeed.

Genesis 3:3
But of the fruit of the tree which is in the midst of the garden, God
hath said, Ye shall not eat of it, neither shall ye touch it, lest ye die.

John 6:50
This is the bread that cometh down from heaven, that a man may eat
thereof and not die.

Genesis 3:22
And the Lord God said, Behold, the man is become as one of us, to
know good and evil: and now, lest he put forth his hand, and take
also for the tree of life, and eat, and live forever. . .

John 6:51
I am the living bread which came down from heaven; if any man eat
of this bread, he shall live for ever: and the bread that I will give is
my flesh, which I will give for the life of the world.

Genesis 3:24
So he drove out the man; and he placed at the east of the garden of
Eden Cherubims, and a flaming sword which turned every way, to
guard the way of the tree of life.

John 6:37
All that the Father giveth me shall come to me; and him that cometh
to me I will in no wise cast out.

Reading Jesus' words to the Capernaum audience brings to mind
the passages in Hebrews in which the Anointed One is shown in a
series of declarations to be superior to the elements of the Old Covenant. Eternal Living Bread, He told them, is superior to temporal
desert bread. The superiorities are listed:

1. The *source* of the Bread of Life (6:33)—"from heaven"
2. The *abundance* of the Bread of Life (6:33b)—"unto the
   world"
3. The *substance* of the Bread of Life (6:35)—"I am the bread of
   life"
4. The *sufficiency* of the Bread of Life (6:35b)—"shall never
   hunger"
5. The *breaking* of the Bread of Life (6:51)—"I will give my
   flesh"

6. The *partaking* of the Bread of Life (6:53)—"except ye eat"
7. The *sustenance* of the Bread of Life (6:54)—"hath eternal life"
8. The *assimilation* of the Bread of Life (6:56-57)—"dwelleth in me and I in Him"

His discourse drew to a close with what is on the surface an enigmatic statement, yet one that is indispensible to our union with "Christ our Passover," who was sacrificed for us. His words laid the foundation for the continuing symbolic memorial to His finished work—the Lord's Table.

"I am the living bread which came down from heaven: if any man eat of this bread, he shall live for ever; and the bread that I will give is my flesh, which I will give for the life of the world" (6:51).

Jesus' statement confounded His listeners, and they "strove among themselves saying, How can this man give us his flesh to eat?" (6:52). To this He replied, "Except ye eat the flesh of the Son of Man, and drink his blood, ye have no life in you" (6:53). His selection of a word was the key to their understanding and ours. Every quotation in the gospels touching the Lord's body being sacrificed (broken) employs the Greek word for "body" (*soma*). Only in John 6 do we find Him using the word for "flesh" (*sarx*). Contextually, the subject was the manna that came down from heaven. Israel, in the desert, raised a complaint: "Give us flesh, that we may eat" (Numbers 11:13). In Exodus we learn, "And Moses said, This shall be, when the Lord shall give you in the evening flesh [quail] to eat, and in the morning, bread [manna] to the full" (16:8). Moses spoke at God's direction. "I have heard the murmurings of the children of Israel: speak unto them saying, At even, ye shall eat *flesh*, and in the morning ye shall be filled with *bread*; and *ye shall know that I am the Lord your God*" (Exodus 16:12, italics added).

Another question was raised in the Passover readings that did not escape our Lord's attention. Thirsty children of Abraham "murmured against Moses, saying, What shall we drink? And he cried unto the Lord; and the Lord showed him a tree, which when he had cast into the waters, the waters were made sweet" (Exodus 15:24-25). On this point Jesus instructed them by confirming, "And he that believeth on me shall never thirst" (6:35).

Israel's three basic physical needs had been met "from above" in the wilderness: drink, bread, and flesh. God's Son, sent from above, provides the spiritual equivalent for His hungry Israelites: He is their *Drink* (6:35), *Bread* (6:48), and *Flesh* (6:54). To partake of these elements would cause the believer to dwell in the Son, and the Son in him (6:56). This vital fusion would accomplish eternal union with Jehovah. "As the living Father hath sent me, and I live by the Father: so he that eateth me, even he shall live by me" (6:57).

Sad to say, Jesus experienced the same difficulties with contemporary Israel as had Moses before Him. "His disciples murmured at it," and concluded, "This is an hard saying, Who can hear it?" (6:60).

All of the facts had been stated by their patient Messiah. But two necessities awaited fulfillment: (1) the historical accomplishing of His coming sacrifice; (2) the consequent compelling ministry of the Holy Spirit, who would "draw" (6:44) those whom "the Father giveth me" (6:37). Shadow had given way to substance. What would their answer be? It came quickly. "From that time many of his disciples went back, and walked no more with him" (6:66). Jewry's problem, then and now, was their stumbling over His pronouncements of personal deity. But not all failed to comprehend.

THE CONFESSION (6:67-69)

We can well wonder what the disciples must have felt as they saw rapture turned into retreat. Those who but short hours before had moved to make Him king were retiring from His presence in search of another. The fuse that flashed with such brilliance had sputtered and died short of a revolutionary explosion. Effects of their own work and witness, which had lifted them to such exhilarating heights, seemed to diminish with the ebbing of the multitude.

After they had watched them go, Jesus turned to His little band. The disciples returned His gaze—it was intent and purposeful. "Then said Jesus unto the twelve, will ye also go away?" (6:67). Peter spoke first—it seemed he always did. His words reflected the conviction of every member of their circle but one. The outspoken fisherman had good reason for his eagerness to be the first to reply to the Lord's question.

On that memorable night of the storm (6:15-25), when Jesus had come walking to them across the ferocious surface, something had happened to Peter. The issue was not so much really what happened *to* him, as what had transpired *in* him. For on that evening the cocksure son of the sea petitioned the Master of wind and water to relieve an impulse most of us have felt at one time or another—to walk on water. The Lord bade him, "Come," and Simon plunged over the side of the vessel and began to walk the whitecaps. He was doing fine, too, "but when he saw the wind boisterous, he was afraid; and beginning to sink, he cried, saying, Lord, save me" (Matthew 14:30). Peter, the man with the determination of a battering ram, was intimidated by the assailing torrent. In one awful instant he became disoriented and endangered. His icy immersion froze his senses in a chill of helpless loneliness. The fisherman's ability to control his situation was as far beyond his grasp as the safety of the distant shore. It was a *doomed man* who was "afraid." It was a thoroughly *desperate man* who shrieked above the blast of the storm, "Lord, save me." It was a *different man* who reentered the boat, drenched but delivered.

A subdued disciple sat relieved and safe amidst his fellows. Yes, he would show flashes of the old thunder and fire, and even failure in future days, but in a transforming way, on that dark night, one drowning fisherman in the hands of his Savior surfaced as an apostle of God.

Appropriately, then, and with a conviction not born of observation but personal interaction, Simon Peter spoke out. "Lord, to whom shall we go? Thou hast the words of eternal life. And we believe and are sure that thou art that Christ, the Son of the living God" (6:68-69).

There is no one else to whom we can go—"Lord, to whom shall we go?"

There is no one else to hear—"Thou hast the words of eternal life."

There is no one else to trust—"We believe, and are sure that thou art that Christ, the Son of the living God."

Such was their response to the Messiah's second Passover. Those eleven believing Jewish hearts articulated their faith in Peter's great confession. He also spoke for others; because even though the multitude departed, there was, as there has always been among the Jewish people, that precious remnant who would be satisfied with nothing less than God's Living Bread.

5

Fire and Water

John 7:2—10:21

Raise the song in festive mood,
For from God's faithful hand
Rain has brought the harvest forth
From out a thirsty land.

"I am here with drink enough
For every son and daughter."
Come ye to the fountainhead—
Jesus is the WATER.

From a distance it appeared the Temple was burning. Great fires could be seen leaping high into the night sky. Light from the flames swept the city with an intensity that seemed to brighten every courtyard in Jerusalem. Worshipers on their way to the nightlong service at the Temple passed strange, leafy little huts standing outside houses, in courtyards, and even on rooftops. Light shone through them, projecting shadowy patterns against the buildings and on the flagstone streets.

The source of the illumination was discovered just beyond the Beautiful Gate, inside the Court of the Women. Four huge golden candelabras, each with four bowls atop it, stood in the court. Young priests joyfully scaled ladders with containers of oil to fill the receptacles, insert cloth wicks, and ignite them. One could hear gasps of delight as the throng was dazzled by the sudden bursts of light. The crowd moved back to make room for the entry of the "men of piety and good deeds." These came into the court, every man holding a torch, and began dancing in circles around the candlesticks, singing songs of praise to Jehovah. Levite musicians holding instruments, harps, lutes, cymbals, and trumpets lined the fifteen semicircular steps that led up to the Nicanor Gate. There they played and sang hymns before Jewish pilgrims who had gathered from all sections of the inhabited world.

Many an enraptured son of Jacob, observing these festivities, must have remembered the words of Isaiah: "Ye shall have a song, as in the night when a holy solemnity is kept; and gladness of heart, as when one goeth with a pipe [flute] to come into the mountain of the Lord, to the mighty One of Israel" (30:29). To many Jewish people, this was called *The Feast.* Tishri's fifteenth dawn had brought to Israel the brightest of all her celebrations. Tabernacles (Sukkot) was upon them, and it was a time of thanksgiving and rejoicing.

TABERNACLES

"Speak unto the children of Israel, saying, The fifteenth day of this seventh month shall be the feast of tabernacles for seven days unto the Lord" (Leviticus 23:34). "On the eighth day shall be an holy convocation unto you; and ye shall offer an offering made by fire unto the Lord: it is a solemn assembly; and ye shall do no servile work therein" (Leviticus 23:36).

The Feast of Tabernacles was divinely established as a seven-day commemoration followed by a one-day "convocation" (Sabbath). In its entirety, it was actually an eight-day observance. The feast embodied three basic elements that involved Israel's past, present, and future.

Her past. Tabernacles was a memorial feast during which the nation was to pause and remember: "That your generations may know that I made the children of Israel to dwell in booths, when I brought them out of the land of Egypt: I am the Lord your God" (Leviticus 23:43).

To enhance their awareness of His deliverance, the people were instructed to take "on the first day the boughs of goodly trees, branches of palm trees . . . and willows of the brook; and ye shall rejoice before the Lord your God seven days" (Leviticus 23:40).

Every household in Israel was obliged to construct a booth from the boughs of living trees. They were to be arranged to provide shade and covering, but not to the extent that sunlight and rain were excluded. With but few exceptions, Israelites were to dwell in their "tabernacles" for the seven days of the feast. These "booths" were to become the actual dwelling places of the people during the celebration. There they would sleep, take meals, meditate, pursue study, and pray. Annually, therefore, Israelites built, according to the rabbinically prescribed requirements, their memorial huts in whatever location they found most convenient.

Her present. "Also in the fifteenth day of the seventh month, *when ye have gathered in the fruit of the land,* ye shall keep a feast unto the Lord seven days" (Leviticus 23:39, italics added).

This was a time for extended national thanksgiving. Crops had been harvested from lands watered by their beneficent God. Tabernacles was Israel's feast of ingathering, attended by proper ceremonial recognition of Jehovah's supply and their expectant supplication for the "latter rains," which would prepare the land for another abundant yield. An ancient rabbi counseled, "Pour out the water at tabernacles, for it is the rainy season, that the rains may be blessed to thee."

Her prophetic future. Scripture dictates that seventy bullocks were to be sacrificed at the feast (Numbers 29:12-40). Bullocks were offered in diminishing numbers—one less each day—over the period of the observance. The Talmud offers the rabbinic explanation: "There were seventy bullocks, to correspond to the number of the seventy nations of the world." In other words, the beasts were offered in anticipation of the last days, when Gentile nations would be gathered to the Messiah. This prophetic aspect will be clarified shortly. Now, however, we note that prophetic foreview was very much in the picture at this feast.

DOMINANT FEATURES OF TABERNACLES

Of the observances peculiar to Tabernacles, two aspects predominate—*illumination* and *water libations.*

We have referred to the giant candlesticks and torch ceremonies marking the opening of the feast. That night of festive celebration concluded with a climactic demonstration and declaration. As dawn approached, two priests entered the Women's Court, sounding their trumpets as they walked toward the Beautiful Gate. Upon reaching it, they turned and facing west toward the Sanctuary said, "Our fathers, who were in this place, they turned their backs on the Sanctuary of Jehovah, and their faces eastward, for they worshiped the sun; but we, our eyes are toward Jehovah.'' Israel's light, they affirmed, was from the Lord and shone from that place of worship to the far reaches of heathendom.

The water libation was of such significance that the Feast of Tabernacles was termed the "House of Outpouring.'' The Jerusalem Talmud ascribes special significance to the ceremony. In addition to the element of thanksgiving and expectation of rain for the harvest, the question is raised, "Why is the name of it called, the drawing out of water? Because of the pouring out of the Holy Spirit, according to what is said: 'With joy shall ye draw water out of the wells of salvation' '' (Isaiah 12:3).

One of the most intriguing acts of worship witnessed by the assembled masses was this outpouring at the Temple. A priest was dispatched daily to lead a procession from the Temple to the pool of Siloam. He carried a golden pitcher and walked to the accompaniment of music until he reached the pool and there filled the vessel with water. The return to the Temple was timed to correspond with the placing of the burnt-offering on the altar. Priests trumpeted his arrival and entrance through the Water Gate into the Court of the Priests. There he was met by another priest, one who was designated to carry the wine (drink) offering. Together they walked up the rise to the altar. Water and wine were poured into two silver funnels. With this act the singing of the Great Hallel began.

At the conclusion of the outpouring, priests would walk in procession once around the altar chanting, "O, then, work now salvation, Jehovah! O, Jehovah, send now prosperity.'' On the last day, "the great day of the feast,'' also called the "Great Hosanna,'' the priest made seven circuits around the altar, as Israel had heathen Jericho long ago. Once again prophetic implications are seen. The Gentiles would one day fall before triumphant Judaism and join with the true worshipers of Jehovah for the great and final outpouring and ingathering.

THE BIBLICAL BACKDROP

We will concentrate on two passages taken from 1 Kings and Zechariah, which are cited as having been special selections read at the Temple and in the synagogues during the Feast of Tabernacles.

Both have historical associations with the feast and very significant relationships to the themes of water and light.

First Kings 8 records the assembly of the elders of Israel "unto King Solomon in Jerusalem, that they might bring up the ark of the covenant of the Lord out of the city of David, which is Zion" (8:1). This was done at the "feast" of the "seventh month" (Tabernacles). Removal of the sacred Ark came with the completion of Solomon's Temple on Mount Moriah—it was the day of the great dedication.

"And it came to pass, when the priests were come out of the holy place, that the cloud filled the house of the Lord, so that the priests could not stand to minister because of the cloud; for the glory of the Lord had filled the house of the Lord" (8:10-11).

The Shekinah glory, Israel's light of all lights, filled the house. Jehovah was "tabernacling" with His people, and He would be made known to them in the hallowed place of meeting. David's kingly son, in the prayer of dedication, petitioned that when "there is no rain, because they have sinned against thee," that confession, repentance, and chastisement would bring reconciliation and righteousness that He might again "give rain" upon His land.

Solomon's benediction extends beyond the borders of Israel in the expectancy "that all the people of the earth may know that the Lord is God, and that there is none else" (8:60).

Zechariah joined David's wisest son with words that gave substance to the king's desire and rang with soul-thrilling reverberations through the ranks of the Israelites gathered at the feast. The prophet envisioned (chap. 14) Israel's final ingathering. Preparations for the culminating feast would begin when Messiah's "feet shall stand in that day upon the Mount of Olives, which is before Jerusalem on the east" (14:4).

Israel's Anointed One will bring unceasing light. "But it shall be one day which shall be known to the Lord, not day, nor night; but it shall come to pass, that at evening time, it shall be light" (14:7).

"And it shall be in that day, that living waters shall go out from Jerusalem" (14:8). (See also Ezekiel 47:1-12; Revelation 22:1-2). Living waters will flow out from Jerusalem perpetually.

Supremely, Zechariah told the nation of the time to come when God, in the person of their Messiah, would dwell in their midst—not to tabernacle, but at last to take up permanent residence as Sovereign over His redeemed people.

In that day:

"Shall the Lord go forth" (14:3)
"And his feet shall stand" (14:4)
"And the Lord my God shall come" (14:5)
"And the Lord shall be King over all the earth" (14:9)

Gentiles will be subdued and join reconciled Israel in the ascent to Jerusalem "from year to year to worship the King, the Lord of hosts, and keep the feast of tabernacles" (14:16).

These readings, taken together, served to prepare Israel biblically for the glorious age to be ushered in at the Messiah's appearance:

1. Messiah-God tabernacling with men
2. Messiah bringing light (revelation) and water (sustenance)
3. Messiah reconciling Israel and reigning over Abraham's seed
4. Israel's final ingathering to the Messiah and the land
5. Messiah's subjugation of the Gentile nations and their future subservience to Him

The divinely chosen selections set before the people yet another illustration of the great gulf existing between biblical and rabbinical Judaism. Furthermore, they provided the scriptural pillar upon which the God-Man would place His credentials. Israel would soon be given a clear choice between priestly rationalizing and divine revelation. John provides an arresting appraisal of the extent of that revelation.

JESUS AT THE FEAST

"Now the Jews' feast of tabernacles was at hand" (7:2).

People were whispering in Jerusalem. Jewry's "holiest and greatest" feast was underway, but the controversial rabbi from Galilee was nowhere to be found. His relatives were in the city and, perhaps, some of His disciples. "But where," they asked, "is He?" The question rang with expectancy among the multitudes awaiting His arrival in the City of David.

Preparations for the journey to Jerusalem provide informative insights into the isolation Jesus experienced while He tabernacled in a world dominated by the prince of darkness. Not only was He a stranger in the house of His "friends," the Messiah was also an alien in His own household, "for neither did his brethren believe in him" (7:5). The Father's heavenly Joseph would know rejection and biting sarcasm from those who were, from a human standpoint, closest to Him. When one understands that Jesus would be facing the religious leaders' resolute commitment to see Him executed (7:1)—this was no secret—His brothers' challenge seems even more callous. "His brethren therefore said unto him, Depart . . . and go into Judea, that thy disciples also may see the works that thou doest" (7:3). "If thou do these things, show thyself to the world" (7:4). Their reasoning was logical and worldly. He must prove Himself in Jerusalem, not among the remote hamlets of Galilee. Go, He was told, to the center of pomp, prestige, and power to make claims of messiahship—see if they would believe on Him there. He would go but not in compliance with their demands. Jesus went up to the feast of Tabernacles, not to *prove* Himself, but to *present* Himself to the nation.

"But when his brethren were gone up, then went he also up unto the feast, not openly, but as it were in secret" (7:10).

As the initial phases of the celebration were being enacted, Jesus was entering Bethany where, we believe, He went into the lodging prepared by Martha, Mary, and Lazarus. His reception into their house contrasted dramatically with the departure from Galilee. Among these faithful friends He was honored, reverenced, and eagerly heard. How like the experience of those who have, because of their belief in Him, been rejected by their own but find a wonderful reception in the family of fellow believers.

The weary traveler would, of course, take up residence in the booth that probably stood in the courtyard of His friends' home. There, in quiet seclusion, Jesus would await the moment of His entrance into Jerusalem and ascent to the Temple. In a very literal way, the Son was "tabernacled" among His people.

It has been suggested, and is probably correct, that the events recorded in Luke 10:38-42 transpired on this occasion. The story provides us a magnificent illustrative microcosm. Lazarus was away looking after the family's religious obligations for the feast. Martha, the scurrying hostess, was busy with necessary but mundane matters. Mary sat at Jesus' feet listening with rapt attention to every word falling from His lips. As Martha hurried through the courtyard in her endless pursuit of serving, she could see Mary through the branches and open portion of the hut, sitting, sitting, sitting. Big sister finally had all that she could take and appealed to her Lord. "Dost thou not care that my sister hath left me to serve alone?" (Luke 10:40). His well-known reply to this one He loved so much (John 11:5) was a response designed not to degrade her activity but rather to rebuke her anxiousness and redirect her priorities. "Martha, Martha, thou art [anxious] and troubled about many things: But one thing is needful: and Mary hath chosen that good part, which shall not be taken away from her" (Luke 10:41-42).

It is all here: the Savior dwelling in a tabernacle of "goodly branches" (Zechariah 3:8; 6:12) unknown to the world, while religionists sharpened swords against Him, and believers who were distracted by ceremonial activity and cumbered with service near and for Him but not preoccupied with Him. Yet, as always, there was a faithful listening remnant, and just beyond the walls of that household many waited to hear and believe.

The steps leading up to Jesus' grand announcement at the Feast of Tabernacles were paved by three questions.

QUESTION 1: "Where is he?" (7:11)

Tabernacles had a very different look that year. An element had been introduced that would divert the attention of people from the festive ceremonies of the feast toward another center of concentration. The question rippled repeatedly through the assembled masses in a guarded undercurrent of conversation. "There was much murmuring among the people concerning him. . . . Howbeit no man spake openly of him for fear of the Jews" (7:12-13). Even before His arrival in Jerusalem, Jesus of Nazareth was the foremost topic of discussion and controversy. "Some said, He is a good man; others said, Nay, but he deceiveth the people" (7:12). Opinion was divided, but one thing was sure: Jesus Christ was the issue at the Feast of Tabernacles.

QUESTION 2: "How knoweth this man letters, having never learned?" (7:15)

Jesus' appearance at the Temple (7:14) and His feast discourses brought astonished reaction. There was in the minds of His hearers only one avenue to the knowledge of "letters": the schools of the rabbis. And since He had not been trained in their theology, how could He possibly be a learned teacher? Their question settled, therefore, on the issues of sources and authority.

The acceptable route to learning followed by the rabbis of Israel was an upward trek. One began by receiving instruction from an esteemed teacher. He then worked back through the pronouncements of the great rabbis, finally reaching Moses and, beyond him, God. In other words, it was current procedure to progress from theological deductions backward toward the ultimate sources of truth, Moses and Jehovah. Jesus, to their dismay, reversed the process and spoke from the Source, divested of the myriad traditions and interpretations standing between the people and their God.

In the course of their verbal exchanges, Jesus leveled charges against the leaders of the Jewish people—accusations cast for illumination against the law they professed to revere.

1. *They sought to kill Him.* "Did not Moses give you the law, and yet none of you keepeth the law? Why go ye about to kill me?" (John 7:19).

2. *They compounded their guilt by professing ignorance of the intent to commit murder.* "Who goeth about to kill thee?" (7:20).

3. *They disregarded their own scriptures about the Sabbath day by circumcising while making it a capital offense to heal on the Sabbath.* "If a man on the sabbath day receive circumcision, that the law of Moses should not be broken, are ye angry with me, because I have made a man. . .whole on the sabbath day?" (7:23).

They had, of course, no legitimate defense to offer, so they threw out a covering diversion. "Thou hast a devil" (7:20). What His enemies could not answer, they would condemn, despite all sound evidence to the contrary.

His point would be driven home when the scribes and Pharisees brought the woman taken in the act of committing adultery (8:1-11). Their appeal to the law of Moses was intended to test Him, "that they might have to accuse him" (8:6). Jesus' answer was given when He "stooped down, and with his finger wrote on the ground" (8:6). Those who conjecture that He listed the commandments make a contextually logical observation. When He issued the invitation

"He that is without sin among you, let him first cast a stone at her" (8:7) they become conscience-stricken and retired from His presence. To the man, His opponents were compelled to agree that "none of you keepeth the law" (7:19).

The Messiah's infinite patience with those who sought His life is an exhibition of divine longsuffering. He *appealed* to them, "If any man will do his will, he shall know of the doctrine; whether it be of God" (7:17). Sincere seekers of truth, He told them, have nothing to fear from Him. Beyond this, Jesus *explained* that He did not come to glorify Himself, but He only sought the glorification of the Father who sent Him into the world. His desire was consistent with those among them who sought nothing for themselves, only glory for their God. Further, the God-Man *reasoned* with them. If Sabbath circumcision is not a breach of Moses' law, why should they indict Him because He had relieved suffering and brought deliverance on the sacred day? Finally, He *besought* that they "judge not according to the appearance, but judge righteous judgment" (7:24). In other words, serve with the spirit as well as the letter, not as executioners, but as true ministers of God.

QUESTION 3: "Do the rulers know indeed that this is the very Christ?" (7:26)

Confusion clouded the Temple atmosphere. Some were wondering why Jesus was allowed to teach openly without being apprehended by the authorities. Some were asking, "Is not this he, whom they seek to kill?" (7:25). They wondered, Did the leaders know something they were not sharing with the people? Others were declaring that Jesus could not be the Christ. "We know this man, whence he is; but when Christ cometh, no man knoweth whence he is" (7:27). Another faction concluded that Jesus was, in fact, the promised Messiah. "When Christ cometh, will he do more miracles than these which this man hath done?" (7:31).

The Pharisees were alarmed when they received information about what was being said. Something must be done quickly. Spies were dispatched to gather incriminating evidence from the statements Jesus was making. Others had been sent to take Him into custody, but why had it not been done? The leaders were infuriated and frustrated even more when Jesus began to speak of His coming

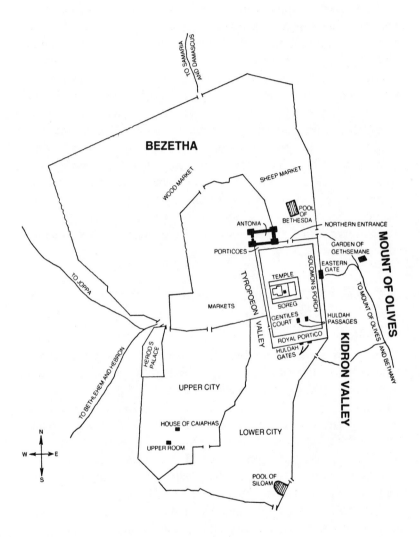

departure. "Yet a little while am I with you, and then I go unto him that sent me. Ye shall seek me, and shall not find me" (7:33-34). Where was He going? they demanded. Was He going to the Jews of the dispersion? Or did He aspire to teach the Greeks? And why would they be unable to reach Him?

Murmurings seemed to be multiplying at the speed of sound when the first rays of light streaked the sky heralding the beginning of the concluding day of the feast.

THE GREAT HOSANNA

Very early on the "great day of the feast" worshipers converged on the Temple mount to join in the climactic celebration of the "Great Hosanna." Jewish people, in splendid attire, came through the gates. Each carried a *lulav* and *ethrog* to be used in the service. A lulav was made of a palm branch that had sprigs of myrtle and willow tied to it by a golden thread. These branches were symbolic of Israel's wilderness booths (Leviticus 23:40). Left hands carried ethrog, a citrus fruit, which symbolized the fruit of the good land God had given them.

Females lining the balconies of the Women's Court strained to see the priestly procession moving slowly through the crowds of pilgrims toward the Water Gate. The golden pitcher, filled with water from Siloam, gleamed in the hands of its priest-bearer. Sharp blasts from the welcoming trumpets sounded as the companion priest, bearing the wine offering, swung alongside for the entry into the Court of the Priests. Eager worshipers had watched the morning sacrifice being arranged on the great altar, which had been bedecked with willow branches. Silver funnels waited to receive the libations carried solemnly toward the base of the altar. In response to calls from the congregants, the priest raised a hand heavenward to signify that the outpouring was taking place.

When the ceremony had been completed, the singing of the Hallel began. Priests chanted lines from the psalms, as the people lifted voices in responsive phrases. Flutes accentuated the swelling Hallelu-Yahs (praise ye the Lord) raised by the multitude at specific intervals. Upon reaching the closing lines of Psalm 118, worshipers joined the euphonious entreaty that marked the grand climax of the service. "Save now. . .O Lord! O Lord, send now prosperity!"

This exclamation was followed by the words "Blessed be he that cometh in the name of the Lord," and, "God is the Lord, which hath showed us light: bind the sacrifice with cords, even unto the horns of the altar" (Psalm 118:26-27).

As the singers approached the closing "Oh, give thanks unto the Lord," they waved their lulavs toward the altar. It has been suggested that the purpose for waving the lulavs was to facilitate remembrance of past deliverances and "to remind God of His promises." Sounds of the exultant refrains slowly died in Temple courts and the valleys of Jerusalem, and a momentary hush descended upon the Sanctuary. This, it is believed, was the precise moment when "Jesus stood and cried, saying, "If any man thirst, let him come unto me, and drink. He that believeth on me, as the scripture hath said, out of his [heart] shall flow rivers of living water" (7:37-38).

Priests and pilgrims alike were frozen by the words ringing through the chambers and echoing off the facade of the Holy Place. Jesus stood before them, the emblems of remembrance in His hands, with words of affirmation flowing from His lips. Jehovah had remembered His promises; the Lord would "save now"; this was, in a way never before realized, "the house of outpouring"—the Messiah of Israel had appeared, and the Spirit would soon be poured out; the hour had come for them to drink of His living water.

The reaction was immediate. "Many of the people therefore when they heard this saying, said, Of a truth this is the Prophet. Others said, This is the Christ. But some said, Shall Christ come out of Galilee? . . . So there was a division among the people" (7:40-41, 43). His announcement stirred a furor among the chief priests and Pharisees. They were enraged by the inconceivable delay in arresting this subverter of the people. Sentiments they could not abide were falling on their ears. One can almost feel the mocking indignation in the Pharisee's remonstrance, "But this people who knoweth not the law are accursed" (7:49). It is of interest that when the leaders could not answer Him, they called Jesus demon-possessed. Now, when they could not dissuade believers in Christ, they accused them of being ignorant rabble, cursed by God.

Conscience, however, would not allow the issue to be put to rest by a shrug of the shoulders and words of derisive condemnation.

They were to hear other voices that day—disquieting voices—not raised from the ranks of the rabble but from those who did know the law. Temple officers sent to take Him returned to their superiors emptyhanded. Their reply to irritated inquiries endures as one of the greatest tributes Jesus' enemies ever paid Him. "Never man spake like this man," they reported. The statement was immeasurably eloquent. Hard on its heels came another assault, one that would undoubtedly linger in the minds of some of them after "every man went unto his own house" (7:53). Nicodemus, the temperate, thoughtful night visitor, would strike the blow. "Doth our law judge any man, before it hear him, and know what he doeth?" (7:51). He was right, of course. The law did not judge a man without a hearing, and they had not heard Him. When Israel's rulers came into His presence, it was ever to argue, never to hear. They had harangued, ridiculed, and plotted, but failed to give the Son of Man a fair hearing. Pharisee and Sadducee alike were being dragged down by the millstone of arrogant presupposition. A fundamental blight was their insufferable conviction of inherent superiority. "Have any of the rulers or of the Pharisees believed on him?" (7:48), they sneered. Their pride had blinded them to any consideration of reasoned inquiry. The superficial non-answer to Nicodemus was a challenge to "search, and look: for out of Galilee ariseth no prophet" (7:52). Priestly scrutiny of the Anointed One was only designed to gather fuel for rebuttal, rebuke, and rejection. It was not judicially objective enough to find out where He had been born.

THE SHINING LIGHT

"These words spake Jesus in the treasury, as He taught in the temple" (8:20). It was probably on what was called the Octave of the Feast, the day following the Great Hosanna, when Jesus taught in the treasury. The treasury, it will be remembered, was located in the Court of the Women. Here, also, stood the giant candlesticks that were so much a part of the celebration of Tabernacles. These silent reminders of God's light shining out from the Temple to the nation and world beyond were in full view when the Messiah issued His second great invitation to the nation. "I am the light of the world: he that followeth me shall not walk in darkness, but shall have the light of life" (8:12).

The time had now come for the Christ to project, in the most manifest way, His light, and in the process expose their darkness. Jesus' words about the light were an extension of His revelation as the Water of Life. His light would lay bare three areas vital to our comprehension of divine purposes: darkness, depravity, and deity.

DARKNESS

At Rosh Hashanah Jesus had brought forth credible witnesses to His deity in a fashion consistent with the requirements of Judaism. Now, in response to the Pharisees' disclaimer (8:13), He told them, "Though I bear record [witness] of myself, yet my record is true" (8:14). They could also be assured that His judgment was "true" (8:16). Both, He says further, are integral elements of the joint testimony He and the Father brought to the responsible representatives of Israel. "I am one that bear witness of myself, and the Father that sent me beareth witness of me" (8:18).

The extent of their darkness is magnified through the questions raised during His discourse. After all Jesus had said and done, they would ask: "Where is thy father?" (8:19) "Who art thou?" (8:25) "Whom makest thou thyself?" (8:53).

A current of malicious accusation flows just beneath the surface of their queries. For although the Pharisees were apparently negligently uninformed about His lineage or place of birth, they seemed quite aware of the rumors circulated about Jesus' conception. They did not ask who His father was but rather, "Where is thy father?" Following this came the taunt, "We be not born of fornication; we have one Father, even God" (8:41). "Say we not well that thou art a Samaritan, and hast a demon?" (8:48). If they were, in fact, so disposed toward Jesus, one can readily understand how their prejudicial preferences would blind them to the truth.

At the Feast of Tabernacles Jesus exposed the rulers':

Darkness concerning the law (7:19, 23)
Darkness concerning the Messiah (7:47-52)
Darkness concerning their sin (8:24)
Darkness concerning His sign (9:24)
Darkness concerning the door (10:1-20)

DEPRAVITY

Jesus' exposition was now reaching the root of their darkness. To the Pharisees, it was unfamiliar territory. They were all aware of the problem of sins, but their spiritual perception was defective when it came to the matter of their possessing sinful natures. There were, they believed, evil inclinations and besetting temptations, but the fact that they were afflicted by inherited sin was a foreign concept. Although man must know that there was a hearing ear and a seeing eye about him, and that his acts were being placed in a book he would face in the future, man could rise above sin by the "study of the Torah and the practice of the precepts." Words placed in Jehovah's mouth by the rabbis proclaimed, "My children! I created the evil inclination, but I have created the Torah as an antidote; if you occupy yourselves with the Torah, you will not be delivered into the inclination's hand." Another word of counsel instructs errant Israelites: "My son, if the impulsive wretch, the *yezar ha-ra* [sinful inclination] attacks you, lead him to the house of learning: if he is a stone, he will dissolve; if iron, he will shiver into fragments."

In answer to their protest "We be of Abraham's seed, and were never in bondage to any man" (8:33), Jesus made a distinction between Abraham's natural seed (8:37) and the spiritual posterity of the first Hebrew (8:39). "If ye were Abraham's children, ye would do the works of Abraham," He told them. To which they replied, "We have one Father, even God" (8:41). "If God were your Father," Jesus continued, "ye would love me." At this point, He articulated the universal problem of those who "are of this world" (8:23). They would do what they did because they were what they were—children of the adversary, alienated from God. Because of their state:

> They refused to hear His truth (8:43-45)
> They sought to kill Him (8:37)
> They were the servants of sin (8:34)
> They would die in their sins (8:24)
> They would be refused God's eternal presence (8:21)

Thus the importance of the answer to their insistent question, "Who art thou?" loomed far larger than they were capable of comprehending. He reveals, in the body of His discourse, two over-whelming truths they must accept.

"Which of you convinceth [convicts] me of sin?" (8:46). They were sinners; He was sinless. Once again, His accusers were at a loss for words. They called Him a "Samaritan" who had a "demon." It has been suggested that the use of the word *Samaritan* at this juncture meant a heretic or even a child of the devil. Perhaps so, but the simple truth is that they failed to face the necessity of a sinless Messiah and their need of a Savior.

"For if ye believe not that I am he, ye shall die in your sins" (8:24). The Anointed One was the exclusive way to the Father. They must exercise implicit belief in His "word" (8:46). Israel's leaders believed that "he only was free who labored in the study of the law." Jesus insisted that continuing in His word would bring them the "truth" that would "make you free" (8:32).

Saving belief would be based on the sacrificial lifting up of "the Son of man" (8:28)—His cross and the affirming evidence of the resurrection—which would cause them to "know that I am He." While this was obviously enigmatic to the rulers, there were those who, as He spoke these words, "believed on him" (8:30).

So we see Christ's sinlessness and saviorhood coupled irrevocably to His coming redemptive sacrifice. These indispensible elements, however, were to be subsidiaries of the one great truth He had come to illuminate at Tabernacles. It is the third but surpassing area in the sequence we have been pursuing.

DEITY

Jesus had been asked, "Art thou greater than our father Abraham, which is dead?" (8:53). "Your father Abraham rejoiced to see my day: and he saw it, and was glad" (8:56), He replied. But, they blustered, this Galilean who stood before them was "not yet fifty years old, and hast thou seen Abraham?" (8:57). It was preposterous to believe that He had seen Father Abraham. In point of fact, Jesus had not said He had seen Abraham, although as the preincarnate Son He certainly had, but that Abraham rejoiced to see *"my day."*

There was current in Israel at this time a tradition believed by many of the leaders and probably known to all of them, that Abraham had seen a vision during his encounter with God recorded in Genesis 15:17. In the vision, it was believed, Abraham had "been shown not only this, but the coming world—and not only all events of the present age but also those in Messianic times." It was quite consistent with their own beliefs, therefore, that Abraham would have seen the days of the Messiah. Yet in the face of Jesus' statement they refused to consider the possibility.

Everything was now prepared. It was a supreme moment of truth. The heavens, it seemed, were hushed and every festive and mundane activity in the universe of God ceased for an instant to hear the sublime declaration *"Before Abraham was, I AM"* (8:58, emphasis added). There could be no mistaking it. The blindest could not be uncertain about what had been declared. Stumble over it they would, but Jesus of Nazareth had finally set forth the fact that He was the preexistent God in flesh—no less that the great I AM.

Now His opponents had all they wanted. They had questioned, accused, and berated Him until He had declared himself. As they cast about for suitable stones with which to pelt the supposed blasphemer, some must have been impressed by the realization that it had not been an intemperate slip of the tongue, induced by their wiles. He had, they knew, intended all along to say it, but it could not possibly be true—could it? Before their resolve became an act, Jesus was gone from their midst.

THE MAN BORN BLIND

To this point Jesus had interacted with the Scriptures and symbolism of the Feast of Tabernacles. His discourses brought emphatic clarity to the issues confronting Israel's leaders and the whole of humanity. Sadly, His message had been swept aside by a hostile tide of opposition. Divine longsuffering, however, has boundaries known only to God. Thus with careful precision the God-Man moved to place a confirming exclamation point behind what He had done and said. Israel would witness the entry of another sign miracle, which would stand before them to demand a decision. It came in the person of a ragged, sightless son of Jacob.

Jesus' subject had been blind from birth and for a considerable period of time had sought alms somewhere near one of the entrances to the Temple. His disciples, reflecting a pharisaic line of reasoning, attempted to establish the cause of his condition. "Master," they asked, "who did sin, this man or his parents, that he was born blind?" (9:2). Jesus' answer gave the divine rationale for what He was about to do. He told them first that neither the man nor his parents were guilty of specific causative transgressions, "but that the works of God should be made manifest in him" (9:3). The imminent miracle was clearly designed to once again verify Jehovah's working through the Son. Jesus had declared His deity; now He would provide the collaborating sign. The miracle displays two distinguishing features.

A CONFIRMATION

"As long as I am in the world, I am the light of the world" (9:5).

The theme of the Feast of Tabernacles was to become the foundation for what Jesus was to do. After He had made clay from saliva and applied it to the beggar's eyes, He sent the blind man away with specific instructions. "And said unto him, Go, wash in the pool of Siloam (which is by interpretation, Sent). He went his way therefore, and washed, and came seeing" (9:7). Siloam was, you will recall, the place where the priest bearing the golden pitcher dipped up the water that so significantly portrayed God's spiritual and physical supply for His land and people. The pool was now to be crowned with the distinction of being associated with Jehovah's Sent One as an affirming sign to Israel. The themes of water and light would coalesce in a pointedly literal fashion as the blind beggar groped to the water's edge, knelt, and applied the cool liquid to his sightless eyes. Slowly, he lifted his head, tiny droplets beading on brows and beard. He opened his eyes and a torrent of light flooded his being. Water and light mingled together as the man blinked away the watery mist and light began to clarify objects, faces, reflections. Jubilantly, he rose to his feet as curious onlookers marveled at what they had witnessed—a man came to the pool blind, had washed, and walked away seeing!

Immediately, the beggar became the subject of an inquiry. Questions were posed by friend and Pharisee. "Is not this he that sat and begged?" (9:8). "How were thine eyes opened?" (9:10). "What sayest thou of him, seeing he hath opened thine eyes?" (9:17). "How then doth he now see?" (9:19). In the end three indisputable facts were established:

1. *He was indeed the man born totally blind.* This was substantiated by the witness of the neighbors, "This is he" (9:9); by his own

admission, "I am he" (9:9), and by confirmation from his parents, "We know that this is our son, and that he was born blind" (9:20).

2. *He now possessed full faculty for sight.* "One thing I know, that, whereas I was blind, now I see" (9:25).

3. *Jesus Christ gave him his sight.* "A man that is called Jesus made clay, and anointed mine eyes, and said unto me, Go to the pool of Siloam, and wash: and I went and washed, and I received sight" (9:11).

Details of the miraculous occurrence could be questioned, but the miracle could not be denied. His work stood in confirmation of His message. It was now the province of Israel's religious representatives to respond.

A CONTRAST

As one reads the reaction of the Pharisees, he cannot avoid observing the contrast of attitude between the Messiah and His persistent adversaries. The rulers offered not one word of congratulation or encouragement for the Jewish brother whose life had been revolutionized by receiving his sight. Very possibly, some of his questioners had dropped coins into his cup when he was blind, but now that he was whole and fit for service to man and God, he was an embarrassment to them. Their thoughts were taken up with *God's Sabbath*—"And it was the sabbath day when Jesus made clay, and opened his eyes. . . . Therefore said some of the Pharisees, This man is not of God, because he keepeth not the sabbath day" (9:14, 16). As was ever the case, they were much more concerned with the day than with a man's deliverance.

There was another telling element: *their superiority.* When the beggar guilelessly asked them, "Will ye also be His disciples?" (9:27) they could not veil their contempt. "Then they reviled him, and said, Thou art his disciple; but we are Moses' disciples. We know that God spake unto Moses; as for this fellow, we know not from whence he is" (9:28-29). The Pharisees were injured, insulted, and infuriated by one who would dare suggest they should stoop to becoming followers of a Galilean.

His heredity and character also fell under their pharisaical scorn. He who was formerly blind had ventured the opinion that God did not hear sinners, but Jehovah did hear those who worshiped Him.

Since his eyes had been opened by Jesus, "If this man," he concluded, "were not of God, he could do nothing" (9:33). By the
way, the man's reasoning was in complete agreement with what
they themselves professed to believe. "They answered and said unto
him, thou wast altogether born in sins, and dost thou teach us? And
they cast him out" (9:34). The poor fellow could have been many
things and been accepted in the synagogue circle. But because he
was the beneficiary of the power and grace of Christ he was no
longer, in their eyes, fit for fellowship.

Contrasting sharply with this attitude was that of Jesus, whose
concern was for the man in the midst of the storm. Whatever higher
designs were being wrought by the God-Man at any point in His
ministry, His heart was filled with selfless compassion for people.
We see a sterling example of it here. Yes, He was presenting His
credentials as God, confronting the nation, and on the way to His appointment with a Roman cross. But above everything else He was
seeking men.

"Jesus heard that they had cast him out; and. . .found him"
(9:35). The man who was cast out, was sought out by Jesus. Where
they faced one another, we are not told. Quite possibly, it was in the
Temple. As the healed outcast looked for the first time at the Lord's
countenance, he heard a question. "Dost thou believe in the Son of
God?" "Who is he, Lord, that I might believe on him?" (9:36).
With these words a beggar prepared to become an heir of the King;
he had arrived at the true summit of his experience. Far more important than his miracle was the identification of his Savior. The
man he had known as "a man called Jesus" and "a prophet" identified Himself. "And Jesus said unto him, Thou hast both seen him,
and it is he that talketh with thee" (9:37). "And he said, Lord, I
believe. And he worshiped him" (9:38).

What Israel's leadership had missed, a blind beggar found. His
day of ingathering had dawned. Tabernacles, for him, was a personal reality. Tragically, God's water for washing and light for seeing
were passed over by those who watched for the nation, and they
would go on serving the symbols.

"And some of the Pharisees which were with him heard these
words, and said unto him, Are we blind also? Jesus said unto them,
If ye were blind, ye should have no sin. But now ye say, We see;
therefore your sin remaineth."

6
A Light in the Temple

John 10:22-39

Windows in the city glow
  With dancing candle flame,
Calling to the pilgrim's mind
  How God's deliverance came.

Comes His word on darkened souls
  To penetrate their night;
Hear Him and you'll find the dawn—
  Jesus is the LIGHT.

"**A**nd it was at Jerusalem the feast of the dedication, and it was winter" (10:22).

Winter's night had descended on Jerusalem. The chill bite of the winds swirling through the valleys reminded Jews of other nights, when a winter of another kind fell with incredible fury on the land and its people. Tiny lights, flickering from every window in the city, penetrated the darkness and warmed the memorial festivities. Israel's severest tribulation had been turned into a resounding triumph. Jewry would pause to pay proper homage to courageous sons and a faithful Sovereign through the Feast of the Dedication, Hanukkah.

Some have questioned why Jesus would make the journey to Jerusalem in order to participate in a feast that was nonbiblical in its origin and, consequently, of scant interest to New Testament students. The God-Man, need we be reminded, never said or did anything that was incidental—every action was monumental. Such was the case when Jesus of Nazareth walked, swathed in winter garments, along Solomon's porch. For on this occasion, though not relating to the symbolism of Old Covenant feasts, He was interacting with Israel's historical past and prophetic destiny. It is an intensely exhilarating display of divine intent. Failure to linger for reverent inquiry into why Jesus attended Hanukkah and what He came to Jerusalem to do will cause one to miss a central view of the larger dimensions of the struggle in which our Savior was engaged while on earth.

A GLIMPSE OF HISTORY

Israel's first Hanukkah celebration was invoked by the Maccabean victory over the forces of Antiochus Epiphanes in 164 B.C. The "dedication" was actually a rededication of the Temple in Jerusalem for the worship and service of Jehovah.

The infamous Antiochus IV and the heroic sons of Mattathias surface in the prophetic writings of Daniel (11:31-32).

"And arms [forces] shall stand on his [Antiochus's] part, and they shall pollute the sanctuary of strength, and shall take away the daily sacrifice, and they shall place the abomination that maketh desolate. And such as do wickedly against the covenant shall he corrupt by flatteries: but the people that do know their God shall be strong, and do exploits."

It was this Antiochus who did, in fact, erect the notorious "abomination of desolation" in the sanctuary, and with his blasphemous action and related atrocities became permanently enshrined in Israel's history as the forerunner of the end-time antichrist.

"THE MANIFEST GOD"

Epiphanes came to the Seleucid throne in the year 175 B.C. to reign over a segment of the empire created by the fallen Macedonian Alexander the Great. Among the provinces he inherited was Judea, with its Temple, curious customs, and baffling devotion to a single God. It was strange indeed, in a world of pagan people and promiscuous gods, to find a nation evincing unswerving allegiance to a solitary, invisible deity. Among the king's initial acts was the appointment of a pro-Seleucid hellenist (advocate of Greek culture) as high priest. Onias III was stripped of his office in favor of a man who after three years was replaced by the radical Menelaus. This arrogant intrusion into a sacrosanct area of Jewish life outraged traditional Jews but was only a harbinger of things to come. Antiochus, in successive edicts, outlawed circumcision, outlawed observing the Sabbath, commanded Jews to apostasize, and designated observing the law of Moses a capital crime. In short, he aspired to destroy Judaism.

A further affront was found in the erection of a gymnasium where Greek athletic games, with naked participants and pregame sacrificial offerings to the gods, lured young priests and other Jewish boys away from their homes and service to God. Enforcement of Antiochus's desires was committed to a garrison of soldiers quartered in the Acra (Citadel), a fortress built on the western hill, across the Tyropeon Valley, opposite the Temple.

The fanatic's crowning offense was the desecration of the Temple in 167 B.C. Antiochus, frustrated by the Jews' adamant refusal to forsake their God, ordered the sanctuary profaned. There is some confusion as to whether the king was himself present for the proceedings. Nevertheless, they were carried out at his bidding. Syrian troops entered the Temple to remove and tear away all remnants of Jewish worship. Then, under the direction of an Athenian philosopher, the building was prepared as a pagan shrine. Jehovah's house was dedicated to the Greek god Olympian Zeus. Above the great altar an image of the mythological deity was hung. One ancient account records that the facial features on the image were in the likeness of the king. Thus in a deliberate act of defiance and self-exaltation Antiochus thrust himself upon the Jewish people as Epiphanes, "The Manifest God."

On the twenty-fifth day of Kislev (December), in commemoration of the sovereign's birthday, the dedication was solemnized by the installation of the "abomination of desolation." A pagan altar was prepared atop the altar of Israel, and a pig was sacrificed on it. The invaders of the sanctuary spattered swine's gore in the Holy of Holies, then brought out the sacred scrolls and threw blood on them before committing them to the flames. In concert with the initiation of worship, licentious pagan rites were performed in the courts. Thereafter, these sacrifices became regular occurrences at the Temple.

This practice, however, became Antiochus's Waterloo. The beginning of the end was waiting for the agents of the monarch in an inauspicious village called Modin, which lay seventeen miles northwest of Jerusalem. Mattathias, a Temple priest, had retired there following the devastation of the sacred place. The old man, flanked by his five sons and surrounded by villagers, went to the town square under orders from one Appelles, Antiochus's official representative, who had come to the hamlet with a detachment of troops. While the soldiers busied themselves with setting up a temporary altar and tethering a pig to its base, the king's emmissary beckoned Mattathias to step from the crowd. The old man had been singled out as the first Jew in the village to thrust a sacrificial knife into a hog. He would then be at the head of the line of townspeople forced to eat the flesh of the tainted animal. The priest stared sullenly into the face of the officer as the people nervously awaited an eruption. It came when a compromising citizen came forward to do the bidding of the Seleucid. Mattathias, livid with rage, leaped upon the man and struck him down. A stunned Appelles was the next to feel his wrath. The sons of the priest-turned-warrior joined the fray, and within minutes it was quiet at Modin once more.

Judah, known as Maccabee (the hammer), and his four brothers led the fight against the forces of Antiochus. These young men and their cohorts faced humanly insurmountable odds. But as surely as the mad king sent his forces to put down the rebellion, they were brought low in a series of stinging defeats. Incensed by his reverses, Epiphanes vowed to exterminate the Jewish people and repopulate their land with pagan settlers. Lysias, regent of the western portion of the empire, along with a superb corps of military commanders and troops, were sent to settle the affair once and for all. Battle was first joined at Emmaus where the confident Seleucids were decisively beaten. Lysias himself undertook an attack on Jerusalem but was routed at Beth-zur. The Maccabeans, with their astonishing victories, had removed the scourge from the land. Clearly acting under the guiding hand of God, Israel's men and boys had met those satanically dedicated to the death of Judaism and Jewry and prevailed.

It was not long until mad Antiochus was carried to his sepulcher. He who crowned himself Epiphanes, "the Manifest God," was in his grave; Israel was alive and well.

LET THE LIGHTS SHINE

The victorious Jews immediately undertook the cleansing of their polluted Temple. As they walked through the weed-infested courts and desolate chambers, tears flowed. Many were so moved that they rent their garments in lamentation. But grief soon gave way to joyful activity as the priests began the construction of a new altar of unhewn stones. Temple vessels, which had been carried away or destroyed by the enemy, were replaced. On the twenty-fifth of Kislev, three years to the day from the entry of the abomination of desolation, the lights burned again in the Holy Place on Mount Moriah. "And the lamps that were upon the candlestick they lighted, that they might give light in the Temple" (1 Maccabees 4:50). The apocryphal books 1 and 2 Maccabees, though properly excluded from the inspired canon of Scripture, provide an excellent historical record of the celebration and origin of Hanukkah.

> Now on the five and twentieth day of the ninth month, which is called the month Casleu, in the hundred forty and eighth year, they rose up betimes in the morning, and offered sacrifice according to the law upon the new altar of burnt offerings, which they had made. . . . Then all the people fell upon their faces, worshipping and praising the God of heaven, who had given them good success. And so they kept the dedication of the altar eight days, and offered burnt offerings with gladness, and sacrificed the sacrifice of deliverance and praise. They decked also the forefront of the temple with crowns of gold, and with shields; and the gates and the chambers they renewed, and hanged doors upon them. Thus was there very great gladness among the people, for that the reproach of the heathen was put away. Moreover Judas and his brethren with the whole congregation of Israel ordained, that the days of the dedication of the altar should be kept in their season from year to year by the space of eight days, from the five and twentieth day of the month Casleu, with mirth and gladness. (1 Maccabees 4:52, 53, 55-59)

Over the centuries a legend arose, which, although fascinating, has obscured the true implications of the feast of lights. The celebration covers eight days, the story has it, with one additional candle being lit each day of the festival because of a miracle that occurred at the dedication. When it was time to kindle the flame on the seven-branched menorah in the Holy Place, the priests found only one cruse of oil that was properly sealed and thus sanctified for use in the Temple. The oil, sufficient for only one day's burning, miraculously lasted over the entire period of the feast. And so the eight-branched Hanukkah candlestick, which we see in Jewish homes and synagogues today, came into being.

Hanukkah lights, however, shine far beyond the realms of quaint stories. They beam away into the regions of manifested deity. When Jesus Christ entered Jerusalem, He brought a greater light, one that illuminated history, revealed prophecy, and flooded believing souls with eternal assurance.

TABERNACLES REVISITED

There can be little doubt that the original observance of Hanukkah was closely allied with the Feast of Tabernacles. Again, the history of the Maccabees, a source close to the event, provides valuable insight. "Now see that ye keep the feast of Tabernacles in the month Casleu [Kislev]" (2 Maccabees 1:9). Another quotation amplifies further: "And they kept eight days with gladness, as in the feast of tabernacles, remembering that not long before they had held the feast of tabernacles. . .therefore they bore branches, and fair boughs, and palms also" (2 Maccabees 10:6-7).

Hanukkah is related to Tabernacles in these words: "Therefore whereas we are now purposed to keep the purification of the temple upon the five and twentieth day of Casleu, we thought it necessary to certify you thereof, that ye also might keep it, as the feast of *tabernacles and of fire*" (2 Maccabees 1:18). This fire is identified as that which descended from Jehovah at the Tabernacle and dedication of Solomon's Temple—Shekinah glory, fiery emblem of the presence of God in the midst of the people of Israel.

Ancient Temple readings for Hanukkah carry through the theme. First Kings 18 was heard during the feast days. Elijah's climactic confrontation with the prophets of Baal is the subject of the portion.

> And Elijah took twelve stones, according to the number of the tribes of the sons of Jacob, unto whom the word of the Lord came, saying, Israel shall be thy name. . . . Then the fire of the Lord fell, and consumed the burnt sacrifice, and the wood, and the stones, and the dust, and licked up the water that was in the trench. And when all the people saw it, they fell on their faces, and they said, The Lord, he is the God; the Lord, he is the God. (1 Kings 18:31, 38-39)

Israel, in the glow of the fire emanating from Jehovah, was called to make a choice between God and Baal. Like alternatives would soon be placed before the leaders of the nation once again.

THE GREAT SHEPHERD

Augmenting the fact of the Lord's presence through the testimonial fire was the assurance that the God who descended was also the One who shepherded His people. Assembled Israelities sat in their synagogues during the feast of lights and heard comforting words from the Scriptures attesting His guidance for a believing people. Attentive ears learned of that better day when the Davidic Messiah will shepherd God's regathered flock. "And David my servant shall be king over them, and they all shall have one shepherd: they shall also walk in my judgments, and observe my statutes" (Ezekiel 37:24). They were instructed that Judah and Ephraim, represented as separate sticks, would "become one in thine hand" (Ezekiel 37:17). Wonderful words these, no more discordant divisions among the sons of Abraham. Union and unity were coming to the people of the Book. But there was an additional word—a rapturously consummating word. "Say unto them, Thus saith the Lord God: Behold, I will take the stick of Joseph, which is in the hand of Ephraim, . . . and will put them with him, even with the stick of Judah, and make them one stick, *and they shall be one in mine hand*" (Ezekiel 37:19, italics added). Israel regathered; Israel redeemed; Israel reunited; Israel rejoicing; Israel reposing—securely resting in the hand of Omnipotence.

"MY SHEEP HEAR MY VOICE"

Jesus went up to Jerusalem with a dual declaration that would shimmer in pristine glory before the flickering lights of Hanukkah. As the Messiah walked among the silent pillars of Solomon's porch, insistent words assailed Him. "Then came the Jews round about him, and said unto him, How long dost thou make us to doubt? If thou be the Christ, tell us plainly" (John 10:24).

The groundwork for what He was about to convey to them had been laid previously. "As I said unto you" (10:26), Jesus reminded them. The phrase looked back to words recorded in John 10:1-21. The subject of the Messiah as the Good Shepherd had been introduced at Tabernacles. Jesus' questioners had had several weeks to turn over the propositions in their minds before they heard afresh the Temple readings and clarifying statements of Christ. Throughout the passage there is an intimacy of association between the

Shepherd-God and His chosen sheep that strains comprehension.

"And the sheep hear his voice; and he calleth his own sheep by name, and leadeth them out. And when he putteth forth his own sheep, he goeth before them, and the sheep follow him: for they know his voice" (10:3-4). The Shepherd, He told them, is also the door through which men must enter. "I am the door: by me if any man enter in, he shall be saved, and shall go in and out, and shall find pasture" (10:9).

Israel's Savior presented the leadership with an exactingly comprehensive view of His shepherding ministry. The Good Shepherd would, He told them:

> Be a Savior—"By me if any man enter in, he shall be saved" (10:9)
>
> Supply abundant life—"They might have life. . .more abundantly" (10:10)
>
> Be sacrificed—"Giveth his life for the sheep" (10:11)
>
> Be a willing sufferer—"No man taketh it from me, but I lay it down of myself" (10:18)
>
> Be the Shepherd of saved Gentiles—"Other sheep I have. . . not of this fold" (10:16)
>
> Be resurrected—"I lay down my life, that I might take it again" (10:17)

Now the Anointed One illuminates the landscape with the grand declaration of the Shepherd-God. "My sheep hear my voice, and I know them, and they follow me: And I give unto them eternal life; and they shall never perish, neither shall any man pluck them out of my hand. My Father, which gave them me, is greater than all; and no man is able to pluck them out of my Father's hand" (10:27-29).

His great shaft of divine light fell fully upon the Shepherd Himself, while at the same time illuminating the benefits of living in the radiance of that Shepherd-light. Believers would experience:

> The light of His life—"My sheep"
>
> The light of His Word—"My voice"
>
> The light of His companionship—"I know them"

The light of His guidance—"They follow me"

The light of His everlasting life—"I give unto them eternal life"

The light of His deliverance from judgment—"They shall never perish"

The light of His strength and security—"Neither shall any man pluck them out of my hand"

The light of His Father's majesty—"My Father. . .is greater than all"

In the synagogue readings we have considered, the weight of emphasis was laid on Israel's reposing securely in the hand of Jehovah. Jesus enlarged and then reduced the scope of the prophecy. It is enlarged to reach beyond the borders of Israel and grasp the whole of humanity. Yet it is not the world en masse or a corporate Israel to which He referred. It is directed toward *everyone,* the world over, who will hear His voice and follow Him. That one believer, and all believers, are held in the sure grip of Christ. It is not, therefore, a matter of our holding on or holding out but rather of the believer's being held by Him.

The light penetrates still further into the night of man's dilemma with Jesus' identification of Himself as the "I AM." "I and my Father are one" (10:30). The Son, the Lamb, the Judge, the Bread, the Light, the Water, the Door, the Savior, the Shepherd, and the willing Sufferer, who would occupy and then vacate a tomb outside the walls of Old Jerusalem, all emerged in a single person—Jesus of Nazareth. He stood before them. And as they beheld Him, they saw the One who was eternally one with the Father—God incarnate. In a vividly pictorial way, the lights of Hanukkah reflected Jehovah's greater light, the sovereign Son.

THE COMING PRINCE

There is another element to be considered, which casts quite another light on why Jesus came to the Feast of the Dedication. It is a point in the presentation of Israel's Messiah where history and prophecy were wed. That which had been lived out and was being memorialized depicted a struggle of larger proportions.

Antiochus Epiphanes came upon the scene as a type of the end-time Antichrist. His suppression of Israel bore all of the characteristics of the coming, infamous usurper—Satan's prince. A brief comparison will be helpful.

1. *Antiochus* had his Jewish champion, Menelaus the high priest, on the scene in Jerusalem, extolling his person and impressing Jews to be obedient to the tyrant. *Antichrist* will have his Jewish false prophet in Israel directing worship to the beast (Revelation 13:11-12).

2. *Antiochus* declared himself divine, desecrated the Temple, and directed worship to himself through the "abomination of desolation." *Antichrist* will enter the Temple, assert his deity, and demand that all mankind, Jew and Gentile, worship at his feet (2 Thessalonians 2:4; Revelation 13:4). He will also set up an "abomination" in the sanctuary (Revelation 13:14-15).

3. *Antiochus* proscribed all worship of Jehovah, making it a capital crime. *Antichrist* will order the execution of all who refuse to worship his image (Revelation 13:15).

4. *Antiochus* marked conforming subjects by forcing them to eat pork and worship at a pagan altar. *Antichrist* will mark by number all who conform to worship at his shrine (Revelation 13:16, 18).

5. *Antiochus* attempted to exterminate Israel's faithful remnant. *Antichrist* will seek to destroy the Jewish people who remain true to Jehovah and refuse to own Antichrist as their sovereign (Daniel 7:22, 25; Revelation 12:13-17; 13:7).

6. *Antiochus* established a fortress in Jerusalem and desired to wrest the land from the Jewish people and repopulate it with pagans. *Antichrist* will establish himself in Jerusalem and attempt to reign over a nation depopulated of believing Jews (Daniel 11:44-45; 2 Thessalonians 2:4).

7. *Antiochus* was defeated by forces pledged to Jehovah and was soon thereafter consigned to his grave. *Antichrist* will be defeated in battle by the Messiah and His army from heaven and be consigned to the Lake of Fire (Revelation 19:11-21).

The essence of the satanic program through Antiochus Epiphanes is succinctly stated by a non-Christian Jewish historian. He wrote, "The reflection is inescapable that had this happened [defeat of Jewish forces], Antiochus might well have succeeded in stifling the

Jewish religion in Judea, and there would have been no dramatic crucifixion of a Jew in Jerusalem two hundred years later" (Moshe Pearlman, *The Maccabees,* p. 75). He is precisely correct. Satan and his human agent conspired to deny the world a *Savior.*

In the case of the Antichrist, Satan aspires to stand on the grave of Israel, in firm possession of God's land, thus thwarting divine purposes in the reconciliation of the Jewish people to their Messiah, delivery of the covenant promises to the people and their land, and circumvent the millennial kingdom's establishment. In other words, Satan and his counterfeit-Christ plot to deny Israel her *King.*

Both propositions, we believe, are in view and confronted by Christ at the Feast of Dedication. Antiochus had attempted to snatch the people and land from Jehovah's hand. God's answer was to raise up and, we must believe, empower the Maccabees to deny his desire. The nation was saved by the hand of God.

In like manner, all of the divine objectives articulated in the prophetic Scriptures, along with Israel's believing remnant, are assured of the perseverance of the promises and people in the eternal plan of God. And, gloriously, the seeds of that coming, consummating harvest were already falling upon the landscape. "And many resorted unto him, and said, John did no miracle: but all things that John spake of this man were true. And many believed on him there" (10:41-42).

"THOU, BEING A MAN, MAKEST THYSELF GOD"

On that day, however, a seemingly impenetrable blindness was upon the custodians of divine responsibility. And although there were some notable exceptions and would in future days be many more, in these hours of critical decision Israel's leadership failed. Jesus had placed before them:

> His works (10:32)
> His word (10:33-36)
> His sonship (10:36, 38)

Their studied response was to:

> Disregard His works (10:33a)

Rebuke Him for His words (10:33*b*)
Revile His sonship (10:32-33)

"Therefore they sought again to take him; but he escaped out of their hand, and went away again beyond the Jordan into the place where John at first baptized; and there he abode" (10:39-40).

And so Jesus passed through the gates of the Holy City on His way to the quiet regions where John had heralded the coming of the Messiah. There He would begin preparations for the final journey to Jerusalem.

7

The Final Sacrifice

John 12:1—20:31

Dark the night that reigned beyond
A small Passover room.
Stricken minds and frozen hearts
Were numbly set in gloom.

Then they heard what we all must,
If we will know God's favor.
Through His finished work we see—
Jesus is the SAVIOR.

THE THIRD PASSOVER

"T hen Jesus six days before the passover came to Bethany, where Lazarus was, which had been dead, whom he raised from the dead" (12:1).

Jesus' arrival for His climactic Passover was an event eagerly awaited by friend and foe alike. Great numbers of local people were anxious to catch a glimpse of the man who had called their neighbor Lazarus from his grave. The brother of Martha and Mary had become an instant celebrity following his exit from the tomb. While curious onlookers came to Bethany, not only to see Jesus, "but that they might see Lazarus also, whom he had raised from the dead" (12:9), chagrined priests plotted to eliminate this source of embarrassment by seeking a way "that they might put Lazarus also to death" (12:10).

Visitors, many of them from Galilee, carefully watched the bands of pilgrims on the roads to the city in the hope of witnessing the entrance into Jerusalem of the Prophet from Nazareth. Conversation in the Temple echoed this interest. "Then sought they for Jesus, and spoke among themselves, as they stood in the temple, What think ye, that he will not come to the feast?" (11:56).

As far as the high priest and elders of Israel were concerned, the matter of the Galilean's threat to their positions had been settled. The council had met and made their decision. An order was issued. "Now both the chief priests and the Pharisees had given a commandment that, if any man knew where he were, he should show it, that they might take him" (11:57).

Never was the atmosphere around Jesus Christ charged as it was on the day of His arrival at Bethany for Israel's final divinely sanctioned Passover. It was an expectancy compatible with the Holy Spirit's objective in bringing readers of John's gospel to an enthralling threshold—one through which we will enter into the true heavenly sanctuary and see the consummation of everything the Lamb came to accomplish. The structure of the closing phases of the gospel of John is a magnificent study in the purposeful precision with which our Guide leads us through Israel's festive seasons and on into the light of the heavenly High Holy Days. And while we shall stand together at the final altar of sacrifice, we shall also be witnesses to the laying of the "cornerstone" from which every "living stone" in the "habitation of God" (the church) would be properly fitted (Ephesians 2:19-22).

John selects, from the flurry of activity during the passion week, those events that were consistent with the carefully defined aims of his gospel. His Spirit-directed development of the revelation unfolding before us falls into five sections:

An Illustration (11:1-57)
Anticipation (12:1-22)
A Summarization (12:23-50)
The Explanation (13:1—17:26)
The Consummation (18:1—20:31)

AN ILLUSTRATION (11:1-57)

The final chapter in the drama of redemption was prefaced by a stupendous sign miracle. Of all of the acts Jesus performed in Judea, it would tower majestically above the rest. There is a sense in which it would cast a confirming gleam of light across the darkened corridors of the final days of the Savior's public ministry.

Lazarus of Bethany, beloved friend of Jesus, had fallen desperately ill. The sick man's sisters, Martha and Mary, directed a messenger to find the Lord and appeal for Him to come to the bedside of Lazarus. Jesus received their communication with a comment to the disciples: "This sickness is not unto death, but for the glory of God, that the Son of God might be glorified thereby" (11:4). His followers, in a few days, would be made aware of the precise nature of that God-glorifying act.

Jesus came to Bethany only after His friend had been dead four days. Martha met her Sovereign with a mild rebuke. "Lord, if thou hadst been here, my brother had not died" (11:21). Her appraisal was shared by friends and neighbors, who later accompanied Mary to the tomb. "Could not this man, which opened the eyes of the blind, have caused that even this man should not have died?" (11:37). Healing was not what the Son of God had in mind, however, and He immediately turned Martha's attention to that fact. "Thy brother shall rise again" (11:23). The woman quite naturally saw this as a future prospect. "I know that he shall rise again in the resurrection at the last day" (11:24).

Her Master led her to the point of the entire episode. "I am the resurrection, and the life; he that believeth in me, though he were dead, yet shall he live: and whosoever liveth and believeth in me shall never die" (11:26-27). The proof and eternal worth of all Jesus had set out to do was clearly projected in these words to a bereaved Martha. He had said it before; now it would be illustrated before ardent believers and adamant critics.

Jesus positioned Himself before the tomb of a man who had been pronounced dead and in his grave for days. Suddenly the silence of the chamber was shattered by the voice of the God-Man. "Lazarus, come forth" (11:43). Astonished watchers heard shuffling movements inside the tomb where only seconds before a lifeless corpse had reposed. They gasped as a form appeared at the opening and stepped out into the sunlight of the land of the living—Lazarus had risen from the dead! Jesus of Nazareth, they now knew, held sway over man's dreaded foe, death. The response, as one would expect, was electrifying. That current, running in one direction, turned on the light. Over another course, it set off an alarm.

"Then many of the Jews which came to Mary, and had seen the things which Jesus did, believed on him" (11:45). His miracle, to these witnesses, was confirmation of what they had heard from the disciple family of Bethany. Perhaps also, on other occasions, they had listened as the Savior Himself spoke words of life. If, they concluded, Jesus could command the dead, He must be the promised Messiah.

"But some of them went their ways to the Pharisees, and told them what things Jesus had done" (11:46). This greatest of miracles laid the final straw on the overburdened animosity of the benighted leadership of the nation. Their reaction will allow us to look past their piously torn garments into the depths of hearts darkened beyond comprehension.

"Then gathered the chief priests and the Pharisees a council" (11:47*a*). The Sanhedrin was in a dilemma. "What do we?" they sputtered, "for this man doeth many miracles" (11:47*b*). Collectively they admitted the validity of Jesus' miraculous activity. There was actually little else they could do. A man who had been dead was now receiving guests into his home. Another, know to most of them, had left a cripple's couch to walk the streets of Jerusalem. And the beggar—that impudent know-nothing—was still looking clear-eyed into the faces of people and inviting them to become disciples of the Nazarene. No, they could no longer attempt to rationalize, debunk, or consign His works to demon empowerment and hope to convince the people that they were right. As much as they detested facing up to it, Jesus of Nazareth did things that mortal men were unable to do.

"If we let him thus alone," one of the elders opined, "all men will believe on him" (11:48). Their admission gave rise to a foundational fear. If He was allowed to continue, everyone would receive Jesus as Messiah and Lord. But why did they fear this? Why not undertake a scrupulous, objective look at His credentials—a thing they had never done—and see if indeed Jesus was the Christ? They would not, because christology and theology were not, after all, their basic concern. Israel's present leadership was obsessed with maintaining place and position. If the nation were converted to Christ and opted for a messianic theocracy, "the Romans shall come and take away both our place and nation" (11:48). And here we find, from the human side of things, that the seemingly inexplicable blindness of the elders was self-inflicted—they refused to look beyond their own interests.

At this point, we are introduced to the wily Caiaphas, Israel's presiding high priest, who was ready with an answer for the problem. He began with a haughty put-down of his contemporaries. "Ye know nothing at all," he said, "nor consider that it is expedient for us, that one man should die for the people, and that the whole nation perish not" (11:49-50). And as Caiaphas settled back to allow his words to penetrate, then to observe the changes of expression, nods, and whispers of agreement, the Holy Spirit invaded the scene to offer the divine explanation. Caiaphas would gladly accept credit for his words and wisdom. But, we are assured, the priest spoke more than he understood. "This spake he not of himself," the Scripture informs us, "but being high priest that year, he prophesied that Jesus should die for that nation" (11:51). Like Balaam of old, who came to curse but was compelled to bless, his determination to destroy would be turned by God into a resolution of redemption. "And not for that nation [Israel] only, but that also he should gather together in one the children of God that were scattered abroad" (11:52).

So while we stand before a full-faced exposure of human rebellion and rejection, for which they bore culpability and would be held responsible, God provides a stunning view of His sovereign competency. The most infamous deeds of men can be turned into instruments of His glory.

The illustration (Lazarus's resurrection) and the reaction (the council's determination to slay Jesus) drew the lines for the coming climactic encounters. "Then from that day forth they took counsel for to put him to death" (11:53).

ANTICIPATION (12:1-22)

Three events are singled out by John to be set forth in anticipation of Christ's present and future work.

First, there was the anointing by Mary in the home of Simon the Leper (12:1-11). This was done at a dinner, apparently a semipublic event, given by Martha, Mary, and Lazarus, but held in Simon's house. "Then took Mary a pound of ointment of spikenard, very costly, and anointed the feet of Jesus, and wiped his feet with her hair: and the house was filled with the odor of the ointment" (12:3).

Hers was an act of understanding and worship. When Mary was rebuked by Judas Iscariot, "Why was not this ointment sold for three hundred pence and given to the poor?" (12:5), Jesus revealed her motive. "Let her alone," He said. "Against the day of my burial hath she kept this" (12:7). The Messiah sat that day under the council's sentence of death. Lazarus, who sat at the table with Him, was also a marked man. "But the chief priests consulted that they might put Lazarus also to death, because that by reason of him many of the Jews went away, and believed in Jesus" (12:10-11). Judas, one of the twelve, was a traitor and a thief (12:6). Even the disciples, who were privy to His innermost thoughts and witnesses to Jesus' confirming deeds, would soon be scattered by the winds of fear and confusion.

But in the midst of the gloom, there was one who understood. Mary had spent time at His feet absorbing reality—not drawing designs for kingdom palaces. She *"sat at Jesus' feet,* and heard his word" (Luke 10:39). In deep distress before Lazarus's tomb, *"she fell down at his feet"* (11:32) and poured out her grief. Now *she knelt at His feet* (12:32) to pour out precious ointment on the One who would soon suffer the agonies of the cross for her and a lost world. In Christ's hour of trial, it was not the luminaries of the apostle band who provided steadfastness, unwavering faith, and supportive worship. It was a small group of godly women who gave themselves quietly to Him as He was giving Himself for us all. Mary's representative act was duly recorded in the account books of heaven. "Verily I [Jesus] say unto you, Wherever this gospel is preached in the whole world, there shall also this, that this woman hath done, be told in memory of her" (Matthew 26:13).

The second event John notes is the entry of Jesus into the city of Jerusalem on the day following His anointing by Mary. "On the next day much people that were come to the feast, when they heard that Jesus was coming to Jerusalem, took branches of palm trees, and went forth to meet him, and cried, Hosanna! Blessed is the King of Israel that cometh in the name of the Lord" (John 12:12-13). The Messiah and the people who accompanied Him from Bethany approached the city along the old caravan road from Jericho. When they reached Bethphage, He sent two disciples with instructions to bring a colt upon which He would complete the journey to Jerusalem. They were descending the Mount of Olives toward the Kidron when a "very great multitude" met the procession. Some began to lay their garments in the way, while others cut down palm branches to spread along the road before the donkey. John observes that these were "people that were come to the feast" (12:12), probably principally people from Galilee and other pilgrims who had heard of Lazarus's resurrection from the dead (12:17-18). The message of the miracle cemented in the minds of many of these the conviction that they were leaving the city to usher in their Messiah, the King of Israel.

The entry into Jerusalem was a fulfillment of prophecy. "Rejoice greatly, O daughter of Zion; shout, O daughter of Jerusalem: behold, thy King cometh unto thee: he is just, and having salvation; lowly, and riding upon an ass, and upon a colt the foal of an ass" (Zechariah 9:9). Israel's King was offering Himself to the nation in accordance with the written prophecies of the Old Covenant. People have questioned the legitimacy of Jesus' offer. In view of the necessity of His going to the cross, was it a genuine offer, they wonder? Yes, it was.

But if such a question has been raised, none have queried the response of Israel's spiritual representatives. "The Pharisees therefore said among themselves, Perceive ye how ye prevail nothing? Behold, the world is gone after him" (12:19). The world? Not really. But whatever direction others might choose to take, it was very evident that Israel's shepherds would not follow Him.

Behind Zechariah's sure word stands another that would thrust itself into the consciousness of Jewry annually until the nation faces her Messiah-King and looks upon the One "whom they pierced" (Zechariah 12:10). The arrow of conviction is found in the phrase "Blessed is the King of Israel that cometh in the name of the Lord" (John 12:13). This quotation is taken from Psalm 118:26 and is among the closing, climactic words of the group of psalms referred to previously, the Hallel. We are reminded that it was sung on the major festive holidays of the nation. It was, therefore, an integral part of national worship. In addition to this, it was recited in every Jewish home (and is to this day) at the conclusion of the annual Passover observance.

When Jesus lamented over Jerusalem (Matthew 23:37-39), He employed the quotation. "Behold," He said, "your house is left unto you desolate. For I say unto you, Ye shall not see me henceforth, till ye shall say, Blessed is he that cometh in the name of the Lord."

A day or two after the Savior had entered Jerusalem, He was again accosted by the chief priests and scribes over the matter of His authority (Luke 20:1-18). His answer came in the form of a parable—the parable of the vineyard. He told them, essentially, two things about Himself. First, He was the "beloved *son*" of the Father, who was slain by the custodians of the vineyard. "This is the heir," they said. "Come, let us kill him, that the inheritance may be ours" (Luke 20:13-14). Second, He identified Himself through a question. "And then he beheld them, and said, What is this then that is written, The stone which the builders rejected, the same is become the head of the corner?" (Luke 20:17). Israel's elite had heard Him, once again, draw from the words of the Hallel. "The stone which the builders refused is become the head stone of the corner" (Psalm 118:22).

The point is that a few days after Jesus and the multitude had announced it, they stood together to sing it. A year later, with the resurrection a reality and a thriving infant church in their midst, they would hear the words ring in the Temple courts, then stand themselves to echo the refrain, "The stone that the builders refused, the same is become the head of the corner," and, "Blessed is he that cometh in the name of the Lord." For the remainder of their natural lives they would hear it, sing it, and remember their infamous deed.

Did the Spirit-implanted seeds of conviction bear fruit? We believe so, for it was later recorded, "And the word of God increased, and the number of the disciples multipled in Jerusalem greatly; *and a great company of the priests were obedient to the faith*" (Acts 6:7, italics added).

The concluding act of anticipation was found in the coming of the Greeks to worship at the feast. "The same came therefore to Philip, which was of Bethsaida of Galilee, and desired him, saying, Sir, we would see Jesus" (12:20-22). Those "other sheep. . .that are not of this fold" (10:16) were in Jerusalem seeking the Shepherd. Not many days hence it could be said that Greek and Jew, circumcision and uncircumcision, barbarian, Scythian, bond and free would find the sheepdoor wide open and rejoicing together enter that fold where "Christ is all, and in all" (Colossians 3:11).

A SUMMARIZATION (12:23-50)

Anticipation now began to flow into a series of preparatory transitions. The introduction to this section of John's gospel brings us to a summary of the feasts visited in preceding chapters. It is not a review but rather a movement in emphasis to the more universal aspects of the feasts in relationship to the Messiah. That is to say, there is a progression from accomplishment in Christ toward future action by the believing beneficiaries of the fulfilling work of the Anointed One.

PASSOVER - FIRSTFRUITS

"And Jesus answered them, saying, The hour is come, that the Son of man should be glorified. Verily, verily, I say unto you, Except a corn of wheat fall into the ground and die, it abideth alone: but if it die, it bringeth forth much fruit" (12:23-24).

This theme was cast in the fact that "the hour is come." Jesus was no longer dealing with prophecy and typology. The time of the great encounter was at hand. Death and resurrection were blood and body to the dawning dispensation. God's expiring Lamb became the falling seed. That seed would spring from the redemptive soil as the "firstfruits of them that slept" (1 Corinthians 15:20). Herein lies the first extension of application. Firstfruits was the time of initial thrusting in of the sickle to reap the harvest standing in the fields. Now the "much fruit" aspect is in view, with the essential relationship between the Lord of the harvest and His reapers articulated. They would experience:

1. *A repudiation of a self-oriented life* (12:25). "He that loveth his life shall lose it; and he that hateth his life in this world shall keep it unto life eternal."
2. *The establishment of committed discipleship* (12:26a). "If any man serve me, let him follow me."
3. *A promise of fellowship* (12:26b). "And where I am, there shall also my servant be."
4. *The prospect of glory* (12:26c). "If any man serve me, him will my Father honor."

ROSH HASHANAH (TRUMPETS)

Jesus brought forth His witness at the Feast of Trumpets in Jerusalem. The confirming voice of testimony from the Father in heaven had been placed before the leadership. Now He spoke again. "Then came there a voice from heaven, saying, I have both glorified it, and will glorify it again" (12:28). The Father's word came in response to Jesus' plea, "Father, glorify thy name." The witness-voice referred to the lifting up of the Son (12:32), which was related to two encompassing events. In complete harmony with the theme dominating the feast, He spoke of judgment. But here He dealt with wider elements. "Now is the judgment of this world: now shall the prince of this world be cast out" (12:31). The future of a world system that is hostile to its maker and the future of the world's "prince," Satan, is sealed. In anticipation of Christ's final triumph, He declares, "He shall be cast out."

Resurrection and life were also important themes for Rosh Hashanah. "And I, if I be lifted up from the earth, will draw all men unto me" (12:32). The word "from" used here actually means "out of." Thus Jesus is speaking at one and the same time of His cross, resurrection, ascension, and exaltation at the right hand of the Father. Through His "lifting up" all men will be drawn toward life in Christ. To be sure, all will not come, but the way will be opened.

TABERNACLES

"Then Jesus said unto them, Yet a little while is the light with you. Walk while ye have the light, lest darkness come upon you: for he that walketh in darkness knoweth not whither he goeth" (12:35).

Tabernacles contrasted the abject darkness of Israel's leaders with the "Light of the world," Jesus Christ. Now He extended the concept. "While ye have the light, believe in the light, that ye may be the [sons] of light" (12:36). Upon Jesus' departure from the earth, a new phenomenon would be displayed: His light would begin to shine out through believing "sons of light." Historically, the lights on the Temple mount were soon to be extinguished. The God-light, however, emanating from the Son and shining through the sons would provide perpetual illumination in a sin-darkened world.

The apostle-author paused at this point to inject an observation and clarification into the text. John wrote, "But though he had done so many miracles before them, yet they believed not on him" (12:37). One can almost hear the sobbing of the man who, humanly speaking, had better comprehension of the mind of Christ than anyone else. They did not believe. Why? It was all so clear, so precise, so complete. Yet they said, "No." Along with the concerned disciple, we are tempted to repeat, "Why?"

There are two sides to the answer. And although, in many respects, they seem to be shrouded in divine mystery, the Holy

Spirit chooses to place them before us. They did not receive Him, "that the saying of Isaiah the prophet might be fulfilled, which he spake, Lord, who hath believed our report? And to whom hath the arm of the Lord been revealed? Therefore, they could not believe, because that Isaiah said again, He hath blinded their eyes, and hardened their heart; that they should not see with their eyes, nor understand with their hearts, and be converted, and I should heal them" (12:38-40).

Isaiah said this, John tells us, "When he saw his [Jesus'] glory, and spoke of him" (12:41). He draws from Isaiah 6, where the prophet sees "the King, the Lord of Hosts," and Isaiah 53, where "the King, the Lord of Hosts" becomes the one on whom "the Lord hath laid the iniquity of us all." So the blinding was done in respect to Christ. Does it mean that God did the blinding in order to make it impossible for them to believe, thus closing some up to receiving His salvation? Of course not. These men made choices for which they were fully responsible. This is demonstrated in the verses that follow. "Nevertheless, among the chief rulers also many believed on him; but because of the Pharisees they did not confess him, lest they be put out of the synagogue; For they loved the praise of men more than the praise of God" (12:42-43). Here is the balance. Some were convinced but would not confess. Their reason: Because they loved the praise of men more than the praise of God. At least two, currently in this state, Joseph and Nicodemus, would later choose to step out for Christ, as doubtless did others. Still, there would be those in that number who would continue to choose the praise of men and would ultimately be as hardened to Him as their peers who had chosen place and position over any consideration of Jesus' claims. Where man's choosing and God's blinding coverge, finite beings are not competent to say. There are, however, certain valid observations that can answer some of our questions.

Was man responsible for his decisions and actions? *Yes.*

Was God sovereign and omniscient in the matter? *Yes.*

Was prophecy fulfilled? *Yes.*

Do we completely comprehend it all? *No.*

DEDICATION

"I am come a light into the world, that whosoever believeth on me should not abide in darkness" (12:46).

At the Feast of the Dedication, Jesus had declared, "I and my Father are one" (10:30). Now He told them, "He that believeth on me, believeth not on me, but on him that sent me. And he that seeth me seeth him that sent me" (12:44-45). Belief in the Father and the suffering Son emerge as a single object of saving faith. Those who believe will "not abide in darkness" (12:46).

A central theme of dedication, we will recall, was that of a delivered people and a deposed tyrant. He moved them on into the realm of final fulfillment with the words "I came not to judge the world, but to save the world" (12:47). He was not contradicting what He had said earlier in His Trumpets statement. He was rather projecting the thought from negative to positive aspects of His ultimate authority. Christ will, assuredly, judge a belligerent world system and depose that system's tyrannical overlord. But keep this ever in mind: He will judge usurpers; He will save His world. This is the rainbow of expectation over creation's present trauma. Individual believers will receive "life everlasting" (12:50). God's world will receive the King.

THE EXPLANATION (13:1—17:26)

IN THE UPPER ROOM

"Now before the feast of the passover, when Jesus knew that his hour was come that he should depart out of this world unto the Father, having loved his own which were in the world, he loved them unto the end" (13:1).

Jerusalem was settling under twilight shadows when Jesus and the disciples climbed the steps to the Upper Room. Upon entering, they found that preparations were complete for His last Passover. Peter and John had been sent into the city with instructions to "prepare us the passover, that we may eat" (Luke 22:8). They obeyed and, bearing their lamb, joined the throng of worshipers at the Temple. How different it was for them this year. They were among their own, but the two followers of Jesus must have felt a distressing sense of isolation. The House of God seemed now to be a haven for the enemies of Christ. Jesus' own words, foretelling the destruction of the Temple and His impending death, weighed heavy on their hearts as they followed the rituals of the sacrifice. In great solemnity the companions in Christ moved away from the Temple courts to wend their way through the narrow streets to roast the lamb and make ready for the seder.

The room was large, festively lighted, and a place where the Lord could share the evening in seclusion with the Twelve. Couches, or pillows, were arranged around a low table. Jewish people reclined rather than being seated around the Passover table. There is some difference of opinion about what memorial objects were on the table at this time. We can, however, speak with certainty about the presence of four items: the lamb, unleavened bread, bitter herbs, and wine. These things would be paramount in the linking of the historical deliverance from Egypt and coming deliverance through the Messiah.

It will at once be noticed that while the Synoptists give us a detailed recounting of the breaking of the bread (His body) and partaking of the wine (His blood), John seems to pass completely over these indispensable details. But when we think back, we remember that he dealt very thoroughly with those elements during the Passover in Galilee (chap. 6). Here the Holy Spirit selectively reveals an aspect of the Savior's ministry that is peculiar to the general purpose of this gospel and the specific immediate intent—conveying clearly the implications of the transitional nature of this supper. Passover was, indeed, that time when the New Testament became an established historical fact. There was expiation for the sinner through faith in His broken body and shed blood, gloriously, eternally. The way to perfect communion was opened between the believer and his God. But there was something else to be seen as well. Not only from God to believer and believer to God, but, also, from believer to believer—ministry within the Body to the Body. It was transmitted through Jesus' washing the disciples' feet.

"He riseth from supper, and laid aside His garments; and took a towel, and girded himself. After that He poureth water into a basin, and began to wash the disciples' feet, and to wipe them with the towel with which he was girded" (13:4-5).

The Lord and Master of all deliberately took the place of a slave and knelt before His followers to wash their feet. While other disciples wondered over Jesus' actions, Peter raised a protest. His statement mirrors the human problems resident in the Upper Room that night. "Thou shalt never wash my feet. Jesus answered him, If I wash thee not, thou hast no part with me. Simon Peter saith unto him, Lord, not my feet only, but also my hands and my head" (13:8-9). The twelve had argued that night. "There was also a strife among them, which of them should be accounted the greatest" (Luke 22:24). Edersheim suggests that the bone of contention was who would have the chief seats at the Passover table. If this was true, Peter may still have been disturbed over his placement, obviously not the nearest to Christ. At any rate, Peter showed: *a lack of unquestioning submission*—"Thou shall never wash my feet;" *he had a human definition of his need*—"Not my feet only, but also my hands and my head;" *a misunderstanding of the divine purpose*—"He that is washed needeth not except to wash his feet, but is entirely clean."

Their once-for-all need, salvation, would be taken care of at Calvary. The perpetual need, daily cleansing, would be provided for along the way. The overwhelming lesson, though, was found in the Lord's example and charge to minister in humility to one another. "Ye call me Master and Lord," He told them, "and ye say well; for so I am. If, I, then, your Lord and Master, have washed your feet, ye also ought to wash one another's feet" (13:13-14). Jesus was not suggesting another ordinance but pressing an example upon them. "For I have given you an example, that ye should do as I have unto you" (13:15). The Master became the Minister. And "the servant. . .is not greater than he that sent him" (13:16).

Look about that room for a moment, through the mind's eye. From a strictly human perspective, it is a depressing sight. After the years of association with Jesus in public ministry; following hundreds of hours of personal instruction by the God-Man; subsequent to their witnessing His triumphant interaction with Israel's prophetic feasts; in spite of all the singular privileges they had enjoyed at Jesus' side, the men nearest Him in life came to that upper room bickering and divided.

For some time it had been apparent that the literal kingdom would be postponed—He had told them so. Jesus was, instead, going up to Jerusalem to die for the sins of the world. Yet in spite of His communication of what lay ahead, they came to those last hours of ministry in spiritual disarray. Their Upper Room controversy had been boiling for some time. James and John's mother had come to the Lord, along with her sons, and requested, "Grant that these my two sons may sit, the one on thy right hand, and the other on thy left, in thy kingdom" (Matthew 20:21). Her petition had occasioned no little scorn from their companions. "And when the ten heard it, they were moved with indignation against the two brethren" (Matthew 20:24). Peter had previously voiced his concern when he asked, "Behold, we have forsaken all, and followed thee; what shall we have, therefore?" (Matthew 19:27). And there in the Upper Room, there was the controversy over who should be the greatest.

Judas, the betrayer, had already "lifted up his heel against" his Master by striking a bargain with the chief priests. "What will ye give me," he had asked them the day before, "and I will deliver him unto you? And they covenanted with him for thirty pieces of silver" (Matthew 26:15). Jesus sent a shiver of consternation through their ranks with His words "Verily, verily, I say unto you, that one of you shall betray me" (John 13:21).

Then there was Peter's resounding, "I will lay down my life for thy sake" (13:37), to which Jesus replied, "Wilt thou lay down thy life for my sake? Verily, verily, I say unto thee, The cock shall not crow, till thou hast denied me thrice" (13:38). Before we are tempted to castigate Peter, we need to view Matthew's addendum to the fisherman's words. "Likewise also said all the disciples" (Matthew 26:35). As for those other followers, He had informed them, "All ye shall be offended because of me this night: for it is written, I will smite the shepherd, and the sheep of the flock shall be scattered abroad" (Matthew 26:31).

What do we say to all this? Were these men unloving? Were they men devoid of common principles? No. They were simply men as men were and are. Think for a moment about what they had asked their Lord:

To sit "one on thy right hand, and the other on thy left hand, in thy glory" (Mark 10:37). Thus they sought prestige.

"Which of them should be [accounted] greatest" (Luke 9:46). Then they sought power.

"We have forsaken all, and followed thee; what shall we have, therefore?" (Matthew 19:27). And what of *compensation?*

Power, prestige, and *compensation.* Every element they desired was sought by men secular and religious. In the eyes of mankind, their seeking was both natural and commendable. The disciples were, with the exception of Judas, honorable men pursuing honorable ends. Their fear of death and flight to avoid arrest was an inherent, some would say God-given, drive toward self-preservation.

But, we quickly counter, although these things are commended by the world, they are not worthy objectives for men moving in the Spirit. The point is, of course, well taken and vital to our understanding of the place to which we have been led in the gospel of John. We said that the scene in the Upper Room was, humanly speaking, in some respects a depressing sight. It was indeed, but we need to linger there in order to learn. Loving, serving, and witnessing for Jesus Christ are not activities of the human intellect, emotion, or will. And we must not delude ourselves by believing that we are somehow made of better spiritual stuff than our disciple predecessors. The trouble with these men was that they were one feast away from spiritual fulfillment. So as we are given a look at the shortcoming of these believing followers, we can begin to properly appreciate the teaching that is ahead for us.

PENTECOST IN PROSPECT

They were still together in the Upper Room when Jesus began to dispel the gloom that had invaded their little circle. Only Judas was missing from the band, having departed to execute his tragic deed.

From the feasts revisited, by way of the Upper Room, John leads us on into projections of Pentecost. Especially noteworthy is the fact that John's gospel does not record Jesus' attendance at the Feast of Pentecost. This, again, is consistent with the Spirit's purpose, because divine fulfillment of that feast was still historically in the future. Pentecost was the time of the outpouring of the Holy Spirit on the church—that once-for-all event in which He would take up permanent residence in and among believers. Pentecost ushers us toward the highest ground upon which saints will stand during their pilgrimage on earth. When we reach the summit, our understanding of God's plan, our position, and our practices will come into sharp focus.

If one can characterize the situation of the disciples in the last section of John's gospel as *depressing,* perhaps the new ground Jesus broke for them should be related to their *possessing.* For now, with man's proclivity for failure in full view, He lay before them the dimensions of the Spirit-life awaiting them just over the darkening horizon. The next four chapters will clarify their new relationship to Christ, the Holy Spirit's indwelling and ministry, and the Father's purposes for the church.

John's summary of Tabernacles in chapter 12 refers only to light. Nothing was said about the water aspect of that feast. The significance of this element was carefully identified in chapter 7. "But this spake he of the Spirit, which they that believe on him should receive: for the Holy Spirit was not yet given, because Jesus was not yet glorified" (7:39). So although there is, appropriately, no record in the gospel of our Lord's attending Pentecost, He affords an encompassing foreview of what will transpire following His being glorified.

The feast is introduced in Leviticus. "And ye shall count unto you from the [next day] after the sabbath, from the day that ye brought the sheaf of the wave offering; seven sabbaths shall be complete: even unto the [next day] after the seventh sabbath shall ye number fifty days; and ye shall offer a new [meal] offering unto the Lord" (Leviticus 23:15-16).

In meticulous fulfillment of the Old Testament type, it was, in fact, exactly fifty days from Jesus' resurrection until the Holy Spirit came like a "rushing mighty wind" (Acts 2:2). Our purpose here is to discuss the era of the Spirit only in foreview. But note that His coming and ministry would not be a mystical coming-and-going, now-and-again affair. His advent would be as literal and historical as was the birth of the Savior in Bethlehem. And as we listen to the words of Christ describing the divine purpose in sending His Spirit into the world, we will find that He is resident in all believers, all of the time. He was sent, among other things, to do a perfecting work in imperfect people. His indwelling is never seen as a reward for a few who have broken through to sanctification. His coming marked the birth of a new dispensation, one in which all true believers would be indwelt at their spiritual quickening by the abiding Spirit of God.

THE BELIEVER'S RELATIONSHIP TO CHRIST

Immediately after the somber announcement of Peter's coming failure (13:38), Jesus said to them, "Let not your heart be troubled" (14:1). With these words He began to delineate reasons they should come into this new and abiding state of spiritual life. He had already told them repeatedly that He was going away. Now He would tell them to what purpose. His first words offered summary assurance:

> "I go to prepare a place for you" (14:2)
> "If I go. . .I will come again, and receive you unto myself" (14:3)
> "That where I am, there ye may be also" (14:3)

Furthermore, Christ will be:

> The way to life—"I am the way, the truth, and the life: no man cometh unto the Father, but by me" (14:6).
> The abiding manifestation of Jehovah—"He that hath seen me, hath seen the Father. . . . I am in the Father and the Father in me" (14:9, 11).
> The resident intercessor for His believing people—"Whatsoever ye shall ask in my name, that will I do, that the Father may be glorified in the Son" (14:13).

Somewhere between the Upper Room and Gethsemane, Jesus paused to add body to His words. Henceforth, believers would know Christ as the "true vine, and my Father is the husbandman [vinedresser]" (15:1). Those who were "clean through the word" (15:3) were to "abide in me, and I in you. As the branch cannot bear fruit of itself, except it abide in the vine; no more can you, except ye abide in me" (15:4).

He is the *source;* believers are the *conductors;* "much fruit" is the *result.* All nurturing (15:1), pruning (15:2), and chastisement (15:6) are exercised to help saints grasp the principles of an "abiding life." This life involves:

> Dependence on God—"Without me ye can do nothing" (15:5).
> Empowerment through Christ-Word provision—"If ye abide in me, and my word abide in you, ye shall ask what ye will, and it shall be done unto you" (15:7).
> Ever-conscious subservience to our Lord—"Herein is my Father glorified, that ye bear much fruit" (15:8).

Enthronement of love—"As the Father hath loved me, so have I loved you. . . . Love one another, as I have loved you" (15:9, 12).

A new intimacy is introduced for those who are "in Christ." "Henceforth I call you not servants; for the servant knoweth not what his lord doeth: but I have called you friends; for all things that I have heard of my Father I have made known unto you" (15:15). Believers are the ambassadors of the King, privy to all His words, works, and ways.

They are chosen—"I have chosen you"
They are set apart for service—"And ordained you"
They are commissioned for the task—"That ye should go"
They are promised a harvest—"And bring forth fruit"
Their fruit will endure—"That your fruit should remain"
Their requests will be honored—"Whatsoever ye shall ask of the Father in my name, he may give it you" (15:16)

To those standing in the rarified air of this divine high ground, the Lord reveals three things: (1) what He expects of them, (2) what they can expect of the world, (3) what He Himself is about to do and how it will affect them.

What Christ expects of the believers. It is direct, simple, unavoidable. "I command you, that ye love one another" (15:17). He does not give us a choice but rather a command. If we are now raised to the position of being His "friends," we must also learn to be friends with other members of the family. This is especially important in view of the fact that saints, lovable and otherwise, have a common enemy who is dedicated to their spiritual ruin.

What believers can expect from the world. "If ye were of the world, the world would love his own; but because ye are not of the world, but I have chosen you out of the world, therefore the world hateth you" (15:19). In this world, Christians will encounter:

Animosity—"If the world hate you, ye know that it hated me before it hated you" (15:18).
Persecution—"If they have persecuted me, they will also persecute you" (15:20).

Reaction to righteous living—"But now they have no cloak for their sin" (15:22).

Rebellion against revealed light—"But now have they both seen and hated both me and my Father" (15:24).

Baseless hostility toward Christ—"They hated me without a cause" (15:25).

Through it all, Christians are given a clear directive. "And ye also shall bear witness [of Christ]" (15:27).

He did not commission His followers to exhibit a self-righteous paranoia or, conversely, a compromising, join-the-world-for-mutual-comfort attitude. They were to recognize the world for what it was and witness to men as they are.

What He was about to do, and how it would affect them. In conclusion, Jesus spelled out, in exceedingly plain terms, instruction about His departure from their midst. "Ye shall not see me," He told them, "because I go to the Father" (16:16). The disciples were, once again, perplexed at the prospect of His departure. "Verily, verily, I say unto you, ye shall weep and lament, but the world shall rejoice; and ye shall be sorrowful, but your sorrow shall be turned into joy" (16:20). Their travail was to be akin to the anguish of delivering a child, "But," He comforted, "I will see you again, and your heart shall rejoice, and your joy no man taketh from you" (16:22).

After consoling them again with the fruits of their continuing union (16:23-24), Jesus declared, "I came forth from the Father and am come into the world: again, I leave the world, and go to the Father" (16:28). They professed to understand what He was saying and claimed that their faith was fortified (16:29-30). How well the Lord understood His followers and reckoned with their frailty, reminding them again of the dark hour approaching (16:32) and offering words of assurance.

"These things I have spoken unto you, that in me ye might have peace. In the world ye shall have tribulation: but be of good cheer; I have overcome the world" (16:33).

THE HOLY SPIRIT'S INDWELLING AND MINISTRY

"And I will pray the Father, and he shall give you another Comforter, that he may abide with you for ever" (14:16).

Jesus had spoken to His own about His eventual physical return to "receive you unto myself" (14:3). In the interim, the church age, He would come to them in the divine person of the Holy Spirit. "I will not leave you comfortless: I will come unto you" (14:18). Pentecost would herald an age unequalled in the history of mankind since the Fall. It was explained in wonderful detail and looks to the day when the omnipotence, omniscience, and omnipresence of the Creator would be at work in every believer the world over.

The Holy Spirit, the third person of the Trinity, was to be the indweller of the saints. "For he dwelleth with you, and shall be in you" (14:17). It was equally true that both Father and Son would join Him in abiding within our earthen temples. This is, in actuality, the climactic purpose of feast fulfillment, and it is beautiful to behold:

"He (the Spirit) dwelleth with you, and shall be in you" (14:17).

"I (Jesus) will come unto you" (14:18).

"Because I live, ye shall live also. At that day ye shall know that I am in my Father, and ye in me, and I in you" (14:19-20).

In this new Spirit life believers experience His:

Omnipotence—All of the saving, supplying, and sustaining resources of the Godhead will be operative "forever" (14:16) within the redeemed.

Omniscience—Direction for daily living will come from God, who knows the future and can direct us from our innermost being.

Omnipresence—The Lord of glory, who reposes in majesty on high, and the eternal Son, who is seated at the Father's right hand, are at the same time tabernacled in every believing sinner on earth and in heaven.

Under the administration of the Holy Spirit, believers are beneficiaries of divine:

Instruction—"But the Comforter, which is the Holy Ghost, whom the Father will send in my name, he shall teach you

all things, and bring all things to your remembrance, whatsoever I have said unto you" (14:26).
Guidance—"When he, the Spirit of truth, is come, he will
guide you into all truth" (16:13).
Ilumination—"Whatsoever he shall hear, that shall he speak;
and he will show you things to come" (16:13).

At the heart of everything in pentecostal expectancy was the clear
declaration that the ministry of the Holy Spirit during the church age
would center in the exaltation of Jesus Christ: "He shall testify of
me" (15:26). "For he shall not speak of himself. . . . He shall
glorify me, for he shall receive of mine, and shall show it unto you"
(16:13-14). Any message, meeting, or ministry that exalts the Holy
Spirit, therefore, is out of step with the purposes of God.

The coming of the Holy Spirit opened vistas of living, loving, and
sharing. The Spirit life is a

Life of love (15:9-14)—Jesus gave the *commandment,* "love
one another"; the Spirit imparts the *capacity* to do it.
Life of joy (16:22-24)—"Ask and ye shall receive, that your
joy may be full." Jesus *filled* the divine storehouse for us;
the Spirit *opens* it to us.
Life of peace (14:27)—"Peace I leave with you, my peace I
give unto you: not as the world giveth, give I unto you. Let
not your heart be troubled, neither let it be afraid." Jesus
obtained and *proclaimed* it; the Holy Spirit *issues* inner
peace.

The sequence love, joy, peace has been arranged to emphasize the
obvious. Paul enumerates the foremost attributes of the Spirit-life
through the believer. "But the fruit of the Spirit is love, joy, peace"
(Galatians 5:22). Every other character trait of the redeemed
emanates from these three basic qualities of life.

Additionally, life in Him is one of *privileged position* (15:12-16),
constructive separation (unto Christ, 15:18-27), and *perpetual fruit-
bearing* (15:1-8).

Life in the Spirit is one of *receiving* and *giving.* It is striking to see
the number of times, five in all, Christ says that the provision-
through-prayer door is to be thrown open to believers. "Ask what

ye will," He declares, "and I will do it." Our asking must, of course, be to the end that "the Father may be glorified" (14:13), consistent with the word of God. "If ye abide in me, and my words abide in you, ye shall ask what ye will" (15:7). But with these positive restraints recognized, He promises to supply our needs in a variety of contexts:

> 14:13-14 relates to faith in and work for the Father and promises—His *strength* for our *tasks*.
>
> 15:7 deals with abiding in the vine and bearing fruit—His *supply* for our *growth*.
>
> 15:16 addresses itself to His commands and our commission—His *winsomeness* for our *witness*.
>
> 16:23-24, 26 is set in the framework of suffering and outward adversity—His *peace* for our *perplexity*.

Spirit-life provision is translated into power for service as attention swings from receiving to giving. "He will testify of me," Jesus says of the Holy Spirit. "And," He goes on, "ye also shall bear witness" (15:26-27). He speaks to the disciples in the immediate inner circle and those who would follow after. The Spirit's work in the world toward the lost is specified in 16:7-11. This ministry will be carried on through the agency of the witnessing church. "Nevertheless I tell you the truth; it is expedient for you that I go away: for if I go not away, the Comforter will not come unto you; but if I depart, I will send him unto you. And when he is come, he will reprove the world of sin, and of righteousness, and of judgment" (16:7-8).

Christ's Spirit-empowered, Word-bearing ambassadors are to be the source of light through whom the Lord will condemn sin, reveal light, and repudiate Satan. The evidences of the Spirit's indwelling are not seen here in relationship to superficial "sign" manifestations. Proof of purchase by Christ is substantiated through a transformation that revolutionizes the believer's conduct. His life evidences a consistent spiritual wholesomeness and bears the unmistakable mark of having been "born from above."

THE FATHER'S PURPOSES FOR THE CHURCH

The Savior next drew aside to offer what has been called His high priestly prayer. Before His attentive Father and in the hearing of His disciples, Jesus lifted eyes heavenward and prayed. His was a prayer to Jehovah for needy followers, but this hour of intercession flew spiritual light-years beyond simply petitioning over needs. It rose, instead, to place a capstone on every type, symbol, sacrifice, and ceremony we have examined. Solemnly, the God-Man articulated the consummating end to which the plan of God for humanity was directed. If the Lord, through Christ's coming and sacrifice, was making possible His reentry into men, His purpose in doing so was not predominantly to facilitate getting some things done through them. It was done to enable saints to accomplish His supreme objective: *that redeemed people might glorify God.* The glory of God is what this prayer was really all about.

"These words spake Jesus, and lifted up his eyes to heaven, and said, Father, the hour is come; glorify thy Son, that thy Son also may glorify thee" (17:1).

The glory of God was His absorbing desire. Peter, James, and John had been on the mountain when Jesus was transfigured, and there He showed them His glory (Luke 9:27-36). Together they had watched and heard Him glorify God in word and work. Jesus' prayer life had been dominated, as they well knew, by giving the Father the glory for all that was being accomplished. This was all done along the pathway of earthly ministry. Now, however, the Savior was about to be lifted up. "I have glorified thee on the earth: I have finished the work which thou gavest me to do" (17:4). His work on the earth was at an end. The sacrificial work to be done in His being "lifted up from the earth" was yet to be accomplished. But before facing the cross, Jesus clarified His heart's desire for the disciples and those who would follow them in faith. He prayed in anticipation of completing the earthly phase of His ministry. "And now, O Father, glorify thou me with thine own self with the glory which I had with thee before the world was" (17:5).

Christ, in His self-emptying *(kenosis)* at the incarnation, laid aside His heavenly glory to be clothed in flesh. Now, in preparation for Jesus' being "glorified in them" (believers), He prayed for the restoration of the Godhead glory, which He bore before the world was created. This is the glory that will shine through the redeemed. Paul grasped it and declared, "Though we have known Christ after the flesh, yet now henceforth know we him no more" (2 Corinthians 5:16). We will know Him, not after the pattern of the days of His poverty, suffering, and humiliation but in His eternal glory. So it is in the effulgence of Jesus' triumph that the apostle says of you and me, "Therefore if any man be in Christ, he is a new creature: old things are passed away; behold all things are become new" (2 Corinthians 5:17)—sons of God, joint heirs with Christ, emmissaries of the light.

The Lord was specific about our relationship to God's glory. First He prayed that He would be glorified *in us*. "And all mine are thine, and thine are mine; and I am glorified in them" (17:10).

Then, He petitioned that His glory be shown *through us*. "And the glory which thou gavest me I have given them. . .that the world may know that thou hast sent me" (17:22-23).

Finally, He asked that He be glorified *with us*. "Father, I will that they also, whom thou hast given me, be with me where I am, that they may behold my glory, which thou hast given me; for thou lovest me before the foundation of the world" (17:24).

In us, through us, with us! Can we fully grasp it all? No, not at this stage. But we can learn the fundamental truth of our existence in time and for eternity: "The chief end of man is to glorify God and to enjoy Him forever."

Although, confessedly, we are beggared in understanding it all, we can appreciate some areas central to what glorifying God means.

The glory that is God Himself. That is the very essence of the person of Jehovah's being—an essence from which His perfections are displayed through His attributes, which, as we examine them, help us to comprehend something of who God is and what He is like.

We have mentioned omnipotence (all powerful), omniscience (all knowing), and omnipresence (everywhere present) in relationship to our Lord. Add to these immutability (changelessness), unity, holiness, righteousness, justice, goodness, truth, love, mercy, and grace, and we will begin to see something of the glory of the eternal deliverer to whom we are eternally joined.

The glory that is due Him. God moves us to give glory to Him. The exercise of praise, adoration, worship, laud, and honor for Himself, His works, and His ways is essential to spiritual wellbeing. Believers are showing symptoms of spiritual sickness when they glorify self, their preachers, places of worship, positions in church or community, prowess in soul-winning, amassed wealth, statistical dominance, or anything that diminishes the glory of the One who is alone deserving of adoration.

His glory shed abroad in a dark world. This has to do with the testimonial aspect of God's glory and our glorifying Him. What did Jesus ask for His church, in order for Him to be glorified in and through her?

He prayed for unity—"That they may be one, as we are" (17:11). "That they all may be one, as thou Father, art in me, and I in thee, that they also may be one in us" (17:21). "That they may be one, even as we are one" (17:22). There are three specific references to unity among believers. Perhaps we can say one for each member of the Godhead—to the end that saints will experience and demonstrate unity "as we are," and become "one in us."

He prayed for believers' joy—"That they might have my joy fulfilled in themselves" (17:13).

He prayed for believers' holiness—"I pray not that thou shouldest take them out of the world, but that thou shouldest keep them from the evil" (17:15).

He prayed for the believers' righteous service—"Sanctify them through thy truth; thy word is truth" (17:17). Sanctify means "setting apart for sacred use."

He prayed for believers to manifest His truth—"That they also might be sanctified through the truth" (17:19).

He prayed that believers would know His love—"And I have declared unto them thy name, and will declare it: that the love wherewith thou hast loved me may be in them, and I in them" (17:26).

Think about it. Our glorifying God bears a striking resemblance to His personal attributes. The people of God will bring glory to God by becoming more like God. We will never become gods, but we must become God-like. To what end are we to become more like Him? "That the world may believe that thou hast sent me" (17:21), and, "I in them, and thou in me, that they may be made perfect in one; and that the world may know that thou hast sent me, and thou hast loved them, as thou hast loved me" (17:23).

It is not, therefore, by mechanism, manpower, or manipulation that God's work is done, but through those who are, in the words of Paul, "blameless and harmless, the sons of God, without rebuke, in the midst of a crooked and perverse nation, among whom ye shine as lights in the world" (Philippians 2:15). When God is given His place, everything else will fall into place and our zeal for God's work and fervor to win a lost world will be channeled to His glory rather than our aggrandizement.

CONSUMMATION (18:1—20:31)

"When Jesus had spoken these words, he went forth with his disciples over the brook Cedron where there was a garden, into which he entered, and his disciples" (18:1).

Jesus "went forth" into the innermost recesses of Jehovah's redemptive sanctuary. What He bore there is far beyond our powers of comprehension. We but stand in wonder and glory in His finishing the work the Father gave Him to do "beyond the veil."

ISOLATION

The writer of Hebrews speaks of the high priest's entry "alone" into the Holy of Holies and likens his ministry in that darkened chamber to that of our great High Priest, Jesus Christ (Hebrews 9). And though Israel's officiating high priests must have experienced an acute sense of just how alone they were before a holy God, no man before Him experienced the intensity of isolation Jesus knew as He approached the day the Messiah would be "cut off out of the land of the living" (Daniel 9:26).

It began when He entered the garden (Gethsemane) "over the brook Kidron." John does not go into the details of the epochal spiritual struggle Jesus was engaged in there. But we note that while He was assaulted by agonies unknown to any who had gone before, the disciples deserted the prayer circle for sleep.

As He roused from their slumber the followers who had pledged to support Him to the death, the sound of heavy footfalls invaded their quiet retreat. Somewhat in advance of the detachment of Pharisees, priests, and soldiers with lanterns held aloft hurried Judas, the betrayer. The psalmist had seen him coming into that garden long centuries before and had recorded the Messiah's reaction: "Yea, mine own familiar friend, in whom I trusted, who did eat of my bread, hath lifted up his heel against me" (Psalm 41:9). The man from Kerioth came with a kiss—a feigned show of affection that forever placed him at the head of the procession of traitors darkening the pages of history.

Judas is a study in human tragedy. He began his association with Jesus of Nazareth in high hope of a better day. Judas was the only Judean among the twelve. Perhaps he felt instinctively some of the prejudices of his region toward Galileans but suppressed them in order to capitalize on the opportunities offered in a movement of the kind he saw developing around the Nazarene. Progressively, though, while his fellows plodded along toward eventual spiritual liberation, Judas was moving farther into the shadows. He would finally fall beneath the weight of his self-forged chains of rebellion, knowing, at the last, remorse without repentance. "I have sinned in that I have betrayed the innocent blood." And the man who walked with Jesus would die a suicide—"and went out and hanged himself" (Matthew 27:3, 5).

Judas was a tormented man who had:

Lived with the burden of a false profession
Passed his days under the threat of exposure as a thief
Watched his aspirations for success, power, and prominence crumble
Sought comfort in coinage
Staggered to his death with Jesus' unquenchable words, "Friend, why hast thou come?" ringing in his ears.

Can we explain a Judas? Probably not. But, sad to say, we see him again in the lives of those who fall prey to the same base elements.

They came for the Prince of Peace with clubs and swords. He asked them, "Are ye come out as against a thief with swords and clubs for to take me?" (Matthew 26:55). The divine Teacher was being treated like a common thief.

Peter blundered boldly when, "having a sword, [he] drew it, and smote the high priest's servant, and cut off his right ear" (18:10). His defense was earnest but ill-advised. The impetuous "man of the sword," who stood ready to fight a multitude, would within hours fall before a frail maiden's words. "This man was also with him," she would say. "I know him not," Peter would lie (Luke 22:56-57). A bit later his words of disavowal were to ring through Caiaphas's darkened courtyard. "I am not [His disciple]," he cried (18:25). The cock's crow came as an arrow of conviction to the heart of Peter.

After He was arrested, Jesus was taken to the house of Annas, father-in-law of Caiaphas and the true power behind the priesthood in Israel. "And led him away to Annas first; for he was father in law to Caiaphas, which was the high priest that same year" (18:13). Annas, you will recall, was the offended party in Jesus' cleansings of the Temple. It was at the bazaars of the sons of Annas where He vented divine wrath on the Temple trafficking.

From Annas He was taken to Caiaphas's palace, where a hastily called meeting of some members of the Sanhedrin would be convened. It was at this hearing that the false witnesses were heard and brought the charge "This fellow said, I am able to destroy the temple of God, and to build it in three days" (Matthew 26:61). It was left to Caiaphas to get to the heart of the matter. He faced Jesus to demand, "I adjure thee by the living God, that thou tell us whether thou be the Christ, the Son of God. Jesus said unto him, Thou hast said." With this admission "the high priest rent his clothes, saying, He hath spoken blasphemy; what further need have we of witnesses? Behold, now ye have heard his blasphemy. What think ye? They answered and said, He is guilty of death" (Matthew 26:63-66). And as their spit, hands, and malevolent renunciations rained down upon Him, their words engulfed the Son of Man in the stark loneliness He Himself had announced. "He came unto his own, and his own received him not."

THE ACCUSATION

The first streaks of dawn were sweeping the sky when the "elders of the people and the chief priests and the scribes came together, and led him into their council" (Luke 22:66). It was a formal meeting of the Sanhedrin, no more impeded by proper Jewish judicial procedure than the first gathering had been. After they had ratified the earlier decision, Jesus was led away to Pilate (Luke 22:71). At this point, John details the events.

"Then led they Jesus from Caiaphas unto the hall of judgment; and it was early. . . . Pilate then went out unto them, and said, What accusation bring ye against this man?" (18:28-29). Pilate stood outside the Antonia and waited to hear their charge. It did not come. They chose another course. They asked Pilate to trust their judgment. "If," they said, "he were not a malefactor, we would not have delivered him up unto thee." The Roman knew the game and decided not to play. "Then said Pilate unto them, Take ye him, and judge him according to your law." "It is not lawful," they countered, "for us to put any man to death" (18:30-31).

The crafty procurator, when he learned their intent, pressed them to be specific. Luke records their charge. "We found this fellow perverting the nation, and forbidding to give tribute to Caesar, saying that he himself is Christ a King" (Luke 23:2). Now Pilate knew he had best look into the matter, so he "entered into the judgment hall again, and called Jesus, and said unto him, Art thou the King of the Jews?" (18:33). Jesus answered Pilate's question with a question: "Sayest thou this thing of thyself, or did others tell it thee of me?" The judge was suddenly on the defensive. "Am I a Jew? Thine own nation and the chief priests have delivered thee unto me. What hast thou done?" (18:34-35).

Jesus answered, "My kingdom is not of this world." He was not implying that there was no literal kingdom to consider, but that His kingdom was not a spears-and-swords competitor of Rome. It would, when it was established, be manteled in divine omnipotence. So Pilate restated his question. "Art thou a king then?" Jesus' response would bring more light to Pilate than he could bear. "Thou sayest that I am a king. To this end was I born, and for this cause came I into the world, that I should bear witness unto the truth. Every one that is of the truth heareth my voice" (18:37).

Pilate's next little statement exposed the failing heart of Rome's jaded paganism. Amid the meandering speculations of the philosophers, trystings of vainglorious gods, rigidity of Roman enforcement, and every-man-for-himself conditions, an obscure official far from Rome would ask, "What is truth?" (18:38). At the moment, from his point of view, it was a cynical brush-off. But with those words, Pontius Pilate became the spokeman for a spiritually destitute world.

The judge brought in his verdict: a thrice repeated "Not guilty":

"I find in him no fault at all" (18:38).
"Ye know that I find no fault in him" (19:4).
"For I find no fault in him" (19:6).

A troubled Pilate would try various ploys to mollify their animosity but not serve their end. Would they accept condemnation, then clemency, with His release in the seasonal goodwill gesture? "Not this man, but Barabbas," they cried (18:40).

Then perhaps scourging would cool the fire of their hate. Jesus' torn body, wrapped in purple and crowned with thorns, was thrust before them. "Behold the man!" he said. "Crucify him. Crucify him!" they screamed (19:5-6).

Throughout the episode, Pilate showed a reluctance to proceed with the trial against Jesus. His examination of Christ had convinced him of the innocence of the Galilean. Also, the contempt he held for the priests and elders must have influenced his feelings. Then, too, Pilate was a superstitious man. His wife had spoken to him of a dream she had had about Jesus and sent word for him to desist from further action against Him (Matthew 27:19). But the foregoing considerations must be weighed against the fact that Pilate was facing the God-Man. Jesus' bearing, demeanor, and His inexplicable refusal to defend Himself or grovel before the judge and plead for His life brought no little trouble to the Roman's mind. "Speakest thou not unto me?" he shouted. "Knowest thou not that I have the power to crucify thee, and have power to release thee?" (19:10). The Son of God informed the procurator that the matter of His death was in higher hands. The words dug even deeper into Pilate's conscience.

During the course of Pilate's exchanges with the priests and Pharisees, he forced the real charge to the forefront. They articulated their accusation after he had pronounced Jesus guiltless for the third time. Only John reports their words, which again expose the central issue in the fourth gospel. "We have a law, and by our law he ought to die, because he made himself the Son of God" (19:7). The Roman learned from their statement what the matter was actually all about. "When Pilate therefore heard that saying, he was the more afraid" (19:8).

Fearing Pilate would release their quarry, the elders decided to strike the final blow. It would be a lesson in the politics of the day for the reluctant governor. "If thou let this man go, thou art not Caesar's friend; whosoever maketh himself a king speaketh against Caesar" (19:12). That was enough. Pontius Pilate understood all too well the implications of their chiding, and the final scene enacted humanity's foulest deed. Favored Jews and pagan Gentiles joined hands and voices before the bleeding Lamb to cry, "Crucify."

> When Pilate therefore heard that saying, he brought Jesus forth, and sat down in the judgment seat in a place that is called The Pavement, but in the Hebrew, Gabbatha. And it was the preparation of

the passover, and about the sixth hour; and he said unto the Jews, Behold your King! But they cried out, Away with him, away with him, crucify him! Pilate saith unto them, Shall I crucify your King? The chief priests answered, We have no king but Caesar. Then delivered he him therefore unto them to be crucified. And they took Jesus, and led him away. And he bearing his cross went forth into a place called the place of a skull, which is called in the Hebrew Golgotha: where they crucified him, and two others with him, on either side, and Jesus in the midst. And Pilate wrote a title, and put it on the cross. And the writing was, JESUS OF NAZARETH THE KING OF THE JEWS. (19:13-19)

BITTER HERBS

This was, indeed, the Savior's "bitter herb" Passover.
In His suffering Jesus tasted:
Betrayal - by Judas
Denial - by Peter
Desertion - by His disciples
Rejection - by Israel's leaders
Humiliation - before a world He came to save
Condemnation - by Pilate
Scourging - by Gentiles
Mocking - by His own people
Now He would mount the rise to the altar and ascend the cross to hang beneath the weight of divine judgment and wrath as the Final Lamb.

BEFORE THE ALTAR

At this juncture John turns the focus toward the interaction between the messianic declarations of the Old Covenant and the historical fulfillment being lived out in Jesus Christ. He has already alluded to two monumental considerations. In 18:32 he refers to a prophecy of the Messiah Himself regarding the events then transpiring. "That the saying of Jesus might be fulfilled, which he spake, signifying what death he should die." The prophecy is recorded in Matthew's gospel. "Behold, we go up to Jerusalem; and the Son of man shall be betrayed unto the chief priests and unto the scribes, and they shall condemn him to death, and shall deliver him to the Gentiles to mock, and to scourge, and to crucify him: And the third day he shall rise again" (Matthew 20:18-19).

It must not go unnoticed that John ascribes an equal degree of inspiration to this statement by Jesus and those of the Hebrew prophets.

Next, we encounter the phrase found in all of the gospels, "But Jesus gave him [Pilate] no answer" (19:9). Here, without a doubt, the prewritten disclosure by Isaiah of the Messiah's suffering settles upon Jerusalem and Calvary. "He was oppressed, and he was afflicted, yet he opened not his mouth: he is brought as a lamb to the slaughter, and as a sheep before her shearers is dumb, so he openeth not his mouth" (Isaiah 53:7). Both Mark 15:27-28 and Luke 22:37 identify the relationship between the crucifixion and Isaiah's prophecy. Jesus said of His coming sacrifice, "For I say unto you, that this that is written must yet be accomplished *in me,* And he was reckoned among the transgressors; for the things concerning me have an end" (Luke 22:37). Mark adds, "And with him they crucify two thieves, the one on his right hand, and the other on his left. And the scripture was fulfilled, which saith, And he was numbered with the transgressors." Jesus is the Sufferer spoken of by the prophet Isaiah. On Golgotha, God's Lamb would:

Be "despised and rejected of men" (53:3)
Bear "our griefs" and carry "our sorrows" (53:4)
Be "wounded for our transgressions, bruised for our iniquities" (53:5*a*)
Have the "chastisement of our peace" laid "upon him" (53:5*b*)
Be smitten "and with his stripes we are healed" (53:5*c*)

Isaiah reminds us that "all we like sheep have gone astray; we have turned every one to his own way, and the Lord hath laid on him the iniquity of us all" (53:6).

All of this was embodied in that form nailed to the tree, the Servant of Jehovah who "had done no violence, neither was any deceit in his mouth" (Isaiah 53:9).

John's next reference is to Psalm 22. "They [the Roman soldiers] said therefore among themselves, Let us not tear it, but cast lots for it, whose it shall be; that the scripture might be fulfilled, which saith, They parted my raiment among them, and for my vesture they did cast lots. These things therefore the soldiers did" (19:24).

The psalmist's verbal portrait of the expiring Lamb rises to join

Isaiah's description as the most detailed records of the crucifixion in the Old Testament messianic prophecies.

"My God, My God, why hast thou forsaken me?" the smitten Son cries (Psalm 22:1; Matthew 27:46). He was "a reproach of men, and despised of the people" (Psalm 22:6; Matthew 27:39-44). "He trusted on the Lord," they called, "that he would deliver him. . .seeing he delighted in him" (Psalm 22:8; Luke 23:35). His "bones," He exclaims, "are out of joint" (Psalm 22:14; 34:20; John 19:33, 36). Weakness and the intense thirst of crucifixion racked His body. "My strength is dried up like a potsherd, and my tongue cleaveth to my jaws" (Psalm 22:15; John 19:28). "They pierced my hands and my feet" (Psalm 22:16; John 19:18). "They part my garments among them, and cast lots upon my vesture" (Psalm 22:18; John 19:24).

John returns to the psalms for his next quotation. "After this, Jesus knowing that all things were now accomplished, that the scripture might be fulfilled, saith, I thirst" (19:28). He had emerged from the darkness of the most excruciating spiritual suffering inflicted on the cross. "All things were now accomplished," and the Savior remembered the psalms. "Thou hast known my reproach, and my shame, and my dishonor: mine adversaries are all before thee. Reproach hath broken my heart; and I am full of heaviness: and I looked for some to take pity, but there was none; and for comforters, but I found none. They gave me also gall for my meat, and in my thirst they gave me vinegar to drink" (Psalm 69:19-21).

Questions have been raised about the significance of the thirst and vinegar. F. W. Krummacher suggests a comparison between the words *I thirst,* uttered by our Lord on the cross, and those raised by the rich man of Luke 16. "And in hell he lift up his eyes, being in torments" and cried for Lazarus, "that he may dip the tip of his finger in water, and cool my tongue; for I am tormented in this flame" (Luke 16:23-24). Jesus had suffered the ravages of the sinner's alienation from God. It is not difficult to believe that this might touch the heart of His cry.

Another thought is worthy of mention. The Son of God, while thirsting physically, was parched the more for a finished work and rest in the presence of the Father.

Another reference followed Jesus' death. It is associated with the breaking of the legs of the two malefactors crucified with Him. "But when they came to Jesus, and saw that he was dead already, they brake not his legs. . . . For these things were done, that the scripture should be fulfilled, A bone of him shall not be broken" (19:33, 36). The phrase is taken from the psalms. "He keepeth all his bones; not one of them is broken" (Psalm 34:20). The Spirit-directed writer was drawing directly from the Torah and the Passover. Exodus gives us a look at that first paschal lamb. "In one house shall it be eaten; thou shalt not carry forth [any] of the flesh out of the house; neither shall ye break a bone thereof. All the congregation of Israel shall keep it" (Exodus 12:46-47). What was commanded for Israel's first Passover lamb, and cast prophetically forward by the psalmist, became a historical fact in the last Paschal Lamb.

A Jewish authority, commenting on the significance of the unbroken bones in the Passover lamb, relates it to "an apotropaic association." *Apotropos* is a term for guardianship in Jewish law. The word itself means "guardian." "The need for an apotropos arises with persons, adult or child, who are unable to take care of their own affairs." If this was the case, it provides a beautiful illustration of the Lamb's work. Our Lamb has passed through the fires of our judgment and condemnation, now serves as the Redeemer-Guardian of the saints, and will conduct us safely home.

The final prophetic word resounded with present and future implications. "But one of the soldiers with a spear pierced his side, and forthwith [immediately] came there out blood and water. . . . And again another scripture saith, They shall look on him whom they pierced" (19:34, 37). Here John echoes Zechariah: "And I will pour upon the house of David, and upon the inhabitants of Jerusalem, the spirit of grace and of supplications; and they shall look upon me whom they have pierced, and they shall mourn for him, as one mourneth for his only son, and shall be in bitterness for him, as one that is in bitterness for his firstborn" (Zechariah 12:10).

Israel stood on a skull-shaped promontory outside the city of Jerusalem two thousand years ago to "look on me whom they have pierced." On a yet future day, the nation will arrive at her Armageddon and look again. But this time, the look will be one of faith. "And they shall mourn for him." It will be the great day of reconciliation, when Israel joins the apostle John to say, "Even so, come, Lord Jesus" (Revelation 22:20).

So that darkest of days is aglow in the Spirit-fused bond between the feast, the Scriptures, and the Living Word. Moses, the prophets, and Israel's psalmists were called forward to make their contributions to the scene.

The Son of God raised His head. His mother, John, and those faithful female watchers pressed forward to hear what He would say. Soldiers, priests, and townspeople were equally attentive. Perhaps, they muttered, He would call for Elijah or His Father. And as they stood with upturned faces, He cried, "It is finished, and he bowed his head, and gave up the ghost" (19:30).

The sound of His voice lingered above the inscription Pilate had placed over Jesus' head—"Jesus of Nazareth, The King of the Jews." That sign was accurate beyond anything the vascillating Roman understood. But he could now have added another line, also in Greek, Latin, and Hebrew.

JESUS OF NAZARETH, THE KING OF THE JEWS AND THE SAVIOR OF THE WORLD!

It was finished at last. Jesus Christ had mounted to the highest arch in the divinely raised structure of sacrificial redemption. The foundation was in the Torah. The prophets reared the columns of messianic hope, and Israel's feasts curved majestically heavenward with embellishing types, symbols, and ceremonies. They converged in culminating fulfillment when the Messiah completed His cross work. And with His words, "It is finished!" He dropped in the keystone. So now it can be triumphantly declared:

"But we see Jesus, who was made a little lower than the angels for the suffering of death, crowned with glory and honor, that he by the grace of God should taste death for every man" (Hebrews 2:9).

THE SIGN

His death accomplished what His life had not. Joseph of Arimathaea asked Pilate for permission to remove the body of Jesus from the cross. Joseph, identified as a secret believer, now overcame his "fear of the Jews" and owned his Lord. His companion, Nicodemus, we believe was a fellow in the faith. Together they bore Jesus' body away. "Now in the place where he was crucified there was a garden; and in the garden a new sepulcher, wherein was never man yet laid. There they laid Jesus" (19:41-42).

The tomb was later sealed on orders from Pilate in deference to the request of the Pharisees. They remembered His promise to quit the grave after three days. It had been many months since they asked Him their first question in the Temple: "What sign showest thou unto us, seeing that thou doest these things? Jesus answered and said unto them, Destroy this temple, and in three days I will raise it up" (2:18-19). It seemed that an eternity stood between that first Passover and the one in progress. In some respects, it almost had. These were older men, old beyond their years, who said to Pilate in requesting a watch for the tomb, "Sir, we remember that that deceiver said, while he was yet alive, After three days I will rise again" (Matthew 27:63). As fretful priests moved away, Roman legionnaires moved toward the garden to take up their vigil—and the world waited.

Mary Magdalene, who loved Jesus in death as she had in life, could not wait for the dawn to come. "When it was yet dark," she made her way to the garden. She was welcomed by an opened door. Quickly she ran from the garden and met Peter and John. "They have taken away the Lord out of the sepulcher, and we know not where they have laid him" (20:2). John says that the graveclothes provided the first witness. "And he stooping down, and looking in, saw the linen clothes lying; yet went he not in" (20:5). Peter, too, saw them. "And the [cloth] that was about his head, not lying with the linen clothes, but wrapped together in a place by itself" (20:7). They were puzzled as they turned their backs and "went away again unto their own home" (20:10).

But godly, loving, faithful Mary waited. No place on earth held more appeal for her than that little garden. She would linger to weep there. "And as she wept, she stooped down, and looked into the sepulchre, and seeth two angels in white sitting, the one at the head, and the other at the feet, where the body of Jesus had lain" (20:11-12). They wanted to know why she wept. "Because," she confided, "they have taken away my Lord, and I know not where they have laid him" (20:13).

She was apparently overcome and turning to leave when she saw a stranger. "Woman," He said comfortingly, "why weepest thou? Whom seekest thou?" Mary thought He must be the keeper of the garden. She would ask Him. "Sir, if thou have borne him hence, tell me where thou hast laid him, and I will take him away" (20:15).

But Mary would not bear away His body that morning—He stood before her!

"Jesus saith unto her, Mary. She turned herself, and saith unto him, Rabboni; which is to say, Master" (20:16) *Jesus was alive!* Mary ran with the news. She "came and told the disciples that she had seen the Lord, and that he had spoken these things to her" (20:18).

That evening, the disciples, together behind closed doors "for fear of the Jews," saw Him. Jesus came "and stood in the midst, and saith unto them, Peace be unto you. And when he had so said, he showed unto them his hands and his side. Then were the disciples glad, when they saw the Lord" (20:19-20). He had been right all along. Remember His words? "And ye shall be sorrowful, but your sorrow shall be turned into joy" (16:20). That joy swept around the glorious announcement and resurrection verification—*Jesus lives, and all is well.* They never tired of hearing or telling the news.

Hear Matthew's eager word of the angelic communication to the wondering band of women. "Fear not, for I know that ye seek Jesus, which was crucified. He is not here: for he is risen, as he said. Come, see the place where the Lord lay" (Matthew 28:5-6).

Mark gives us another picture. "And he saith unto them, Be not afrighted: Ye seek Jesus of Nazareth, which was crucified: he is risen; he is not here: behold the place where they laid him" (16:6).

Luke joins the circle with phrases that have been memorialized in song and sermon for two millennia. "Why seek ye the living among the dead? He is not here, but is risen" (Luke 24:5-6)!

Evidences continued to flow out from the scriptural accounts and confirming testimonies of believing saints who joined Thomas at the feet of the risen Savior to declare their faith—"My Lord, and my God" (20:28).

Thus a commissioned church ("As my Father hath sent me, even so send I you" [20:21]) Spirit-indwelled (20:22), and bearing a message embued with power to save men from sin (20:23) moved out to confront the world with the proclamation and evidences of the gospel of the grace of God, recognizing and relying upon the sufficiency of the Word of God to draw men, Jew and Gentile, to Christ.

"And many other signs truly did Jesus in the presence of his disciples, which are not written in this book: but these are written, that ye might believe that Jesus is the Christ, the Son of God; and that believing ye might have life through his name" (20:30-31).